P9-DWG-566

THE RESERVOIR TAPES

ALSO BY JON MCGREGOR

Reservoir 13

This Isn't the Sort of Thing That Happens to Someone Like You:
Stories

Even the Dogs

So Many Ways to Begin

If Nobody Speaks of Remarkable Things

THE RESERVOIR TAPES

Jon McGregor

Catapult  New York

Copyright © 2017 by Jon McGregor
First published in the United Kingdom in 2017 by 4th Estate
First published in the United States in 2018 by Catapult (catapult.co)
All rights reserved

ISBN: 978-1-936787-91-3

Catapult titles are distributed to the trade by
Publishers Group West
Phone: 866-400-5351

Library of Congress Control Number: 2017964529

Printed in the United States of America
10 9 8 7 6 5 4 3 2 1

THE RESERVOIR TAPES

1: Charlotte

Could you

I'd like to hear about that day, before anything happened.
Just, from the beginning.

You'd been staying in the village for how long?

And you'd come back because the previous visit had gone so well,
last summer?

And you knew the Hunter family. You got on with them.
So it was an easy decision, to come back for a winter break.

Was it warm enough, in the cottage? I mean, the weather had been wet.
It's quite small, isn't it, the cottage. Lovely. But small.

Sorry, barn conversion.

Had you been on any excursions? Had you gone for any walks?

So you were maybe starting to feel a bit cooped up.

Tell me about that morning.
Did you all have breakfast together? Who was up first?
This might sound trivial, but what would Becky have had, if she was eating breakfast alone?

I know

But these details. They help to build a picture.

If you could

Okay. And then did you come downstairs before she finished her breakfast?

And was that when the idea of going for a walk was discussed?

It would be fair to say that Becky's response wasn't positive, would it?

Is it okay if I call her Becky?

She wasn't enthusiastic about the walk. And the weather wasn't great, at that point.

So you let the matter rest for the time being. To avoid a conflict.

And then the two of you had your breakfast together, you and your husband? Something more elaborate, because you were on holiday, because you wanted to treat yourselves?

But this wasn't a special occasion. Other than being a holiday morning. You weren't celebrating anything.

No.

You made a start on your breakfast, you made some coffee— maybe you read the paper? You were having the newspapers delivered while you were staying in the cottage, is that right?

Barn conversion.

Which newspaper?

And Becky—she'll have gone back up to her bedroom? Or put the television on?

Could you

could we

if we could just talk a little bit about Becky. If you could describe her for me. In your own words. What she was like when she was younger. How she's changed from being a child to being a young teenager. What her—gifts are, if you like. Any challenges there have been. Anything she has found difficult. Anything that comes to mind.

I know

I know this is difficult

this must be very hard for

of course.

So, just to pick up again.

This was the third day of your stay in the village; the idea of a walk had been raised but the weather was looking unsuitable. Becky had got up early, and had breakfast before you. What did she do during the rest of the morning? Had she brought any homework with her?

She was friendly with the Hunters' daughter, I understand. Did she spend any time with her that morning?

Do you know if she was friendly with any of the other young people in the village?

And you knew about that at the time?

Had you met any of those young people when you were staying here last summer? Had you seen them when they came up to the Hunters' property?

There was one boy in particular who Becky became quite close to, wasn't there: James?

I know she's only thirteen, yes.

I wasn't implying

But he wasn't someone you were aware of.

Not at the time.

So, that morning, Becky went across to the Hunters' house, and you assumed she was spending some time with their daughter Sophie.

And she's someone who makes friends easily, would you say? Back at home, is she sociable, does she have a range of friends?

Are there any you've been uncomfortable about her associating with? Have her friendship groups changed recently?

Does she spend much time on the Internet?

Do you monitor that, at all?

So she was with Sophie, and by late morning she still hadn't come back. But you had no cause for concern, you had no reason to think they'd gone far. The weather was still wet at that point, wasn't it?

And the original idea for the walk had been to get out before lunchtime, but with the weather you'd put that on hold.

And late in the morning you went across to fetch Becky, from the Hunters' house. Did you speak to either of Sophie's parents?

Both of them? So Sophie and Becky were there by themselves?

Just Becky, by herself?
Did you think the Hunters would have minded that?

Sophie and her parents had been gone all morning, as far as you knew. Becky hadn't seen them leaving?

Were you surprised by this, were you concerned? How long have you known the Hunters?

Would you describe them as friends?

If we could

to keep to

So you had lunch, the three of you, together. And there was some discussion about how Becky had spent the morning, was there?

How would you characterize her response?

So there was some tension.

Of course.

Well, that's teenagers.

And is Becky someone comfortable with her own company, would you say? Back at home, would she often spend time by herself in that way, that you know of?

So were you concerned that her behavior that morning was out of character, that there might be something else behind it?

But you didn't discuss that with her. You put it down to being on holiday, being in a different environment; just . . . usual teenage restlessness. You got lunch ready.

And for lunch you had?

By this point the weather was improving; the rain had stopped, the sky was clearing, and the idea of a walk was suggested again. A decision was made.

I know.

A decision was made, and immediately after lunch you began to gather a few things together, look at a map, make a plan. Can I ask what you took with you?

So you weren't planning on it being a long walk. You didn't think it worth taking extra waterproofs as a precaution, snacks, a flask?

No, of course, and

No.

Can I ask how well you know the area? Are you experienced walkers, would you say?

But this was a route you'd walked in the summer, when you were here before? You'd followed that same path, from the visitor center, up the hill towards the rock formations on the ridge?

Black Bull Rocks, right.

And had Becky been with you on those occasions? Would you say it was a route she was familiar with?

But on this occasion she was reluctant.

Perhaps we

I'm curious

Did you do a lot of walking when she was younger? Would you say the reluctance on this occasion was more around the tensions between you, rather than the walk itself?

11

Would you describe Becky as fit and healthy? Does she do any sports?

So the walk shouldn't have been a problem for her.

I do realize this must be

of course

and

If we could just go through the sequence of events.

The three of you got into the car, your car, soon after lunch. So this would have been

Two p.m. Okay. And the weather was clear. You'd asked Becky to wear something more suitable on her feet, but she'd refused and you didn't want to start another argument.

That's understandable.

You drove a short distance to the visitor center and parked in the car park there. That would have taken, what, five minutes, ten?

Was the visitor center open? Did you see anyone there?

Were there any other cars in the car park?

So you parked near the main building, and went through the gate by the display board, following the track which leads diagonally up the hill towards Black Bull Rocks.

I realize you've already

I just would

it does help

Did you have a map?

Because it was a route you knew. And you can see Black Bull Rocks almost from the car park in any case, can't you? So it was a simple walk. It was going to be a short walk.

Did you know how long you were expecting it to take?

Did you know what time it was going to get dark?

Had you looked at a weather forecast?

Did you have a phone with you?

Had you planned

No, of course

No

I do realize

It is

it's actually rather misleading, isn't it, the walk up to Black Bull Rocks? The path isn't as direct as it looks from the bottom of the hill. There are several narrow gorges or valleys on the way. The path drops down steeply and climbs up out of each of these.

They call them cloughs, locally, don't they?

And the streams through each of these are running high at this time of year, so it's not always a simple matter getting across them. The ground can be quite boggy down there?

And with the shoes Becky was wearing.

Did she struggle at all?

Struggle.

I mean, if she was having difficulty getting across the streams, keeping her feet dry. Did she express any discomfort or irritation, any reluctance? Did she ever want to stop, or go back?

And did you wait for her, at that point? Did she catch up?

But you at least kept her in sight?

What were your feelings by then, if you don't mind me asking?

That's understandable. Of course.

My daughter was that age not so long ago, I know how

Of course.

Was there any discussion between the two of you about cutting the walk short? Given the conditions, and Becky's behavior?

Was there any disagreement between the two of you, would you say?

And by this point you're how far up the track, how close to Black Bull Rocks?

And had there been any change in the weather?

So you had no reason to be concerned?

How were you finding the conditions? You were wearing more suitable footwear, presumably? You had kept dry up until then?

And had you seen anyone else, had you passed anyone on the track, had you seen anyone in the distance?

Now

this will, I understand

I'm sorry

Can you be clear about when you first realized Becky was out of sight?

And you assumed

she was coming up the steps out of the clough? You were not long
out of it yourselves?

How far behind would you say she was when you saw her last?

I realize

of course

you have, I know

But we agreed, didn't we, that this would be

a chance

a chance for you to put your side of the story.

Obviously I know you'll have been through all this with the police, many times, I do appreciate

I do

But people have questions. Not just locally. People are

It would be helpful to clarify

It would be helpful to hear it from you. People would appreciate that.

Is this?

Can we?

No, absolutely. None of this will

You can decide, afterwards, you can reconsider.

I just want to help you tell your side of the story.

Absolutely.

So. If we can

You realized she was out of sight. You waited. She didn't appear. You had already talked about cutting the walk short anyway so

one of you wanted to

You waited, and she didn't appear. You went back to the top of the path leading up out of the clough, the valley, and you couldn't see her there.

And you called for her, presumably?

You looked to see where she was, if she might be hiding?

At what point did you start to actually become concerned?

And the weather was turning?

How long would you say you were looking before you decided to fetch help?

And your phone

So you had to come back

You came down

And you

This is

I know

I'm sorry

Could you

are you able to say what happened next?

2: Vicky

The first Vicky knew about it was when the girl's parents came bursting into the pub.

The two of them were both talking at once and it took a minute to work out what they were saying. They couldn't find her, was the gist of it.

Their anoraks were covered in mud, so it wasn't much of a leap to guess they meant someone was missing on the hills. Tony had Mountain Rescue on the phone while they were still getting their breath back. Vicky could feel herself tensing up, the way she did, now, at any mention of emergency services.

She's thirteen, they said. Her name's Becky. We only lost sight of her for a moment and then she vanished. We've looked everywhere.

Tony told them Mountain Rescue were asking for locations, and they didn't seem to have a clue. They'd been trying to get to Black Bull Rocks, they told him.

Vicky was sitting near the bar, with Graham. Black Bull Rocks was at the far eastern end of the ridge, above the visitor center, where Vicky and Graham worked. Graham caught her eye. In this weather? they were both thinking. At this time of year?

Some of the people who came here had no idea what they were doing on the hills. Vicky dealt with a fair number of them at the visitor center: people who didn't know how to read a map, or think to check the weather forecast. People who assumed there would be a mobile-phone signal when they got lost. At least if they called in to the center there was a chance to set them straight. It was the ones who marched straight past they had to worry about. And she did worry, often.

Tony held the phone away from his ear and said Mountain Rescue were asking for a description, and the parents looked stumped for a minute.

She's about this tall, the father said, holding his hand just beneath his chin. Dark blond hair, down to her shoulders. No glasses. She looks older than thirteen. She's wearing a white hooded top and a navy-blue body-warmer. Black jeans and canvas shoes.

Canvas shoes.

The mother wasn't saying anything much. She looked lost. She looked like someone who had just stood next to a loud noise and was waiting for her hearing to come back.

Tony got finished on the phone and said things would get sorted quickly now, and not to worry. Someone from Mountain Rescue would be in and wanting to take them out in the Land Rover, he said. He told them there was a back room available, so they could sit in peace. He nodded at one of the other staff to sort some drinks, asking them what they wanted.

Her name's Becky, the mother suddenly said. Becky Shaw. Rebecca, really.

Don't worry, Tony said, as he started leading them off. They're good lads, Mountain Rescue. They know what they're doing. They'll find her.

Vicky thought he might regret saying that. She had a bad feeling already. She got these feelings. It really wasn't Tony's place to go offering that kind of a promise.

*

Of course, people started talking then, once Tony had the parents in the back room. The family had been staying up at the Hunters' new barn conversions, Irene said. She remembered the girl from

23

back in the summer. Irene did the cleaning for most of the holiday lets in the village, and she tended to pick things up as she went. She said the family were from somewhere down south, and she wasn't sure what the parents did but they seemed like the professional type. Both of them working, so the girl must have been used to going off on her own. She spent a lot of time with Sophie, the Hunters' daughter. Same age, give or take.

Martin Fowler chipped in and said he remembered the two of them hanging around the village as well. Used to see them with the Broad lad, he said, and Sean Hooper's son, and what's his name, Deepak. She was a live wire, someone else said. There was talk of them messing around at the reservoirs. They'd been seen swimming at the quarry.

This type of conversation went on for a while.

One thing Vicky had learned when she moved up here was that people liked to talk. Information got around quickly, and if people didn't have actual facts they seemed very capable of filling in the gaps. She'd more than once had to deny being pregnant, after being seen with orange juice in the pub. Saying she didn't drink wasn't enough of an answer. Eventually she'd just announced that she was a recovering alcoholic every time someone tried to buy her a pint. That usually put a stop to the questions.

Assumptions were made about her and Graham as well. We're just colleagues, actually, she often had to say. We've known each other awhile, we're good friends, but that's all. People sometimes had an infuriating way of nodding patiently when she said this, but she'd learned to let it go.

*

She'd known Graham for a long time. They'd been at college together, when they were younger. They'd studied conservation management, but when the course finished he was the one who moved up to Derbyshire and found actual conservation work. She moved down to London instead, where she worked in bars, went to a lot of parties, and got into a bit of trouble. They kept in touch, on and off. He told her about the work he was doing for the national park, and encouraged her to visit. She told him stories about what she was up to in London. She'd thought they were funny stories, at the time, but his responses often involved asking if she was really okay.

She never knew how he'd found her in the hospital. She just knew that each time she woke up, and remembered what had happened all over again, he was there. He told her he'd thought something like this was going to happen, and she told him there was no need to be a smart-arse about it.

It hurt when she laughed, for a long time.

People asked, later, what it had felt like to be in a car crash, and she had to say that she had no idea. It wasn't frightening. She didn't feel any pain. She was lifted out through the window of her car. She was wet all over, and very cold. There were flashing blue lights. She could remember getting into a fight at a party, but nothing after that. There were a lot of fights, in those days. She wasn't a good person to be around. People around here wouldn't believe it, if they knew.

By the time she got out of the hospital, Graham had persuaded her to leave London and move up here. He told her she needed to clear her head, to get back to doing something she loved and get some fresh air in her lungs. He didn't really take no for an answer. She was surprised by his directness, and she went along with it because she didn't know what else to do. He was the only one who'd come to see her in the hospital.

*

Usually, when the Mountain Rescue team got up on the hills, they found who they were looking for. They were all local, and they knew the place like their own backyards. They had a good sense of which way people would head when they got lost and in a panic. They knew where people would try to hide when the weather closed in, and where the likely falling places were.

But this was starting to turn out differently.

Vicky and Graham had been asked to open up the visitor center, for use as an operations base, and over the course of the evening it kept getting busier. The police arrived, and a second Mountain Rescue team was called in. When Vicky brought fresh pots of coffee into the room where they'd spread out the maps she heard someone talk about expanding the search zone, which she guessed meant they had very little idea where the girl might be. It was going to be a long night. There were flashing blue lights outside, and helicopters overhead.

At one point Vicky saw the girl's parents again, being escorted into the map room by a police officer. They weren't in there for long, and were soon escorted out again and into a waiting car. A ripple of silence followed them through the building, as though people were afraid to say the wrong thing in their presence. She'd seen something like this before. The way people kept their distance, as if grief were contagious.

She wanted to go out to the car and tell them they weren't alone. But they were, of course.

She realized that *grief* was probably the wrong word to use about what was happening just yet. But it had been hours already and the weather was only getting worse.

Irene arrived later in the evening, carrying bags of shopping into the tiny kitchen at the back of the visitor center. Right then, she said, unpacking the bags. It's Vicky, isn't it? I've got enough here for six dozen bacon cobs. I'll slice, you spread.

She looked over at Graham, standing behind Irene. He shrugged, making a face to say that there was no point arguing. They'd got the hang of doing this, communicating with glances and nods, over the heads of colleagues and members of the public. They'd reached a kind of understanding. He passed her the butter, and reached up for the frying pans.

*

By morning there were police vans parked all along the verges down the lane. The road had been closed, and there were torch-lights flashing through the beech wood across the way. There were dogs barking.

Graham and Vicky were outside, taking a break, sheltering from the rain under the entryway roof. The blue lights and the police radios were making her think of the night of the accident again. Graham asked if she was okay. She looked at him. She wanted a cigarette. She wanted a drink.

I'm fine, she said. Tired.

That would seem reasonable under the circumstances, he said.

They watched more cars pulling into the car park. A helicopter passed by overhead.

I've arranged for the Cardwell team to come and take over, he said. I think we've done our share. Could I perhaps interest you in some breakfast?

She smiled. She was very cold. Yes, Graham, she said. You can interest me in some breakfast.

*

When they got to the house, Vicky took a shower while Graham started cooking. She was trembling and she felt a little sick and she knew she needed to eat. These were her vulnerable moments. They'd talked about these at the group. She felt bad for worrying about herself, with everything that was going on, but she also knew she had no choice. At the group they talked about putting on your own oxygen mask first.

While she was drying herself she felt dizzy and she had to sit down. Graham had lent her an old fleece and a pair of walking trousers to wear. They smelled musty and they were too big but they were at least clean. She felt comfortable in them.

In the kitchen Graham was just putting the breakfast out on the table. The radio was on and they were talking about the missing girl.

Suits you, he said, glancing up at her outfit. She sat down.

She wanted to say something about the girl's mother. She could feel her eyes starting to sting. She looked at him. There was a question in his expression but she couldn't read it.

Tea's in the pot, he said.

3: Deepak

The morning after the girl disappeared there were police going up and down the street, and journalists setting up in the market square. Deepak's mum said there was no way he was doing his paper round that day.

It's not safe, Dee Dee, she said. We don't know what's happening. You're staying at home now. Anyone could be out there.

His mum still called him Dee Dee, sometimes. No one else dared.

His dad said there were that many police out there, the street was the safest place to be. He said people would be disappointed if they didn't get their papers, and he opened the door for Deepak while the two of them were still arguing about it. Deepak headed out.

It was dark outside, and cold. He got his bike out of the shed. There was a misty drizzle that felt like it would soon turn to rain. He pushed his scarf up over his mouth and rode down to the shop to collect the papers. There were people everywhere. He usually had the street to himself, this early. He heard someone say there was a search being organized, up at the visitor center.

On the news, the police had said they wanted people to keep their eyes open. They wanted to know about anything unusual, any suspicious behavior, any changes in routine. Any detail could help, they said; no matter how small. It felt like they were talking to him personally. If there was anything to notice, he'd notice it. He was good at that. He knew about people's routines. When he was doing his paper round he could always tell who was still in bed, who was having breakfast, who had gone out to work already; he noticed when anything was different. They should make him some kind of detective. Detective Chief Inspector. D.C.I. Deepak had a ring to it.

The Jackson house was the first on his round. Usually a couple of the Jacksons were out in the yard, moving sheep around in the stock shed or loading up the trailer. There was always a smell of bacon and cigarettes, and they never said hello. Place was quiet this morning, though. That was one change in routine to make a note of already.

Irene's house was next, back up the main street. Her son had special needs and went to a different school. Her lights were always on when he got there, just like this morning, and there was always steam coming out of the tumble-dryer vent under the kitchen window, just like there was now. She was an early starter. Nothing to see here.

The butcher's shop was empty. Mr. Fowler would usually be behind the counter, setting everything out, and would shout hello as Deepak pushed the paper through the letter box. He was friendlier than some. Deepak's dad thought it was funny that he kept offering to stock halal meat for the family. He'd stop him in the street and go, Vijay, listen, it's no trouble at all. And Deepak's dad was always like, mate, we're not even Muslim, we don't really eat meat. And then Mr. Fowler would forget, and offer again the next time.

After the butcher's he crossed the square to the pub, the Gladstone, which took four papers. The square was full of police vans and journalists and people just standing around. But there was nothing he could say was suspicious. He carried on up the back lane to Mrs. Osborne's house. It was steep, and the gears on his bike kept slipping. When he got there Mrs. Osborne opened the door, as always. Usually she asked if he had any good news for her, like the news was his responsibility or something. But today she just smiled in that old-person sad way and took the paper.

He rolled back down the cobbles and across the square. D.C.I. Deepak had nothing of note to report. He headed up the main

33

street towards the edge of the village, and as he turned into the lane past the allotments he hit a pothole and his chain came off.

Calling headquarters: request mechanical assistance. Would be cool if he could do that. He got off and started fixing the chain back on. He wondered what the police really meant by something unusual, or something suspicious. They said any detail could be vital, but how would you know? Would it be some piece of clothing, like a lost glove on a railing, or like a hair band in the gutter? Or would it be if you saw someone dodgy in a van? Or something really bad, like a tiny bloodstain, or a strand of hair?

It must be pretty hard being a detective.

It was pretty hard being a bike mechanic as well. The chain was wedged between the frame and the sprocket, and he couldn't get it out. He took his gloves off to try to get a better grip. It was too cold for this kind of thing.

The front door of the house on the corner opened and a man came out. Deepak had seen him around, but he didn't know him. The man asked if he needed a hand, and Deepak said no, thanks, he was fine. The man stood and watched. It was well awkward. The chain was totally jammed, and he couldn't get it shifted. It was cutting into his hands when he pulled at it. The man was just watching. It was embarrassing. He was standing too close.

Deepak, lad, he said; I'd say that chain's stuck. I'll get some tools.

He went back into the house. Deepak wondered who he was. He pulled at the chain again. Time was getting on.

The man came back out with a toolbox, and budged Deepak out of the way. He said it wouldn't take a minute. It was all about having the right tool for the job, he said, and gave Deepak a funny look as though he'd told a joke.

He asked if Deepak was surprised that he knew his name. When Deepak said yes, he said: Well, I've seen you around. You stand out a bit around here.

He did something with a screwdriver and got the chain sorted. It took less than a minute. Deepak said thanks, and went to get back on his bike.

The man said: Hang on there a minute, let's just pop inside and get you cleaned up.

Calling headquarters again: Request guidance. Request backup.

The guidance was obvious. Going into a stranger's house was one of the things you weren't supposed to do. But this man wasn't exactly a stranger; he knew Deepak's name, and Deepak had seen him around. But even so. He could basically hear his mum shouting at him as he walked towards the front door: You don't even know this man, Dee Dee! It's not safe, Dee Dee!

She worried too much, though. His dad always said that.

A real detective would take certain measures in this situation. There would be a colleague waiting in a car farther down the road. A uniformed officer covering the back door. He would be wearing a wire. As it was, he took mental notes. Just in case. A description of the car parked outside, and the registration number. A description of the house. For example: there were piles of junk mail and free papers just inside the front door. The curtains in all the upstairs windows were closed. The man was wearing a waxed jacket, and trousers with lots of pockets. He was old. Sixty, at least.

Deepak knew he shouldn't be going inside. But he didn't want the man to think he was rude, or ungrateful. And anyway, what would he say? I don't want to come inside in case you're some kind of massive nonce? You couldn't go around saying that.

He felt the man's hand on his shoulder, steering him through the door.

Just head through to the back, he said. Kitchen's straight ahead. Soap's by the sink.

It was dark in the hallway, and he had to squeeze past a line of coats and jackets hanging along the wall. Everything smelled damp, and muddy.

This was definitely a bad idea.

He went straight to the sink and started washing his hands. The water was cold, and the bar of soap cracked in half as soon as he picked it up. The sink was full of old dishes. The oil wouldn't come off. It was just making the two halves of soap filthy. He could hear the man doing something in the hallway. The water coming off his hands was black and going all over the dishes, but the oil wasn't shifting. He was making a mess of the man's kitchen. He wanted to leave now. He was going to be late.

He heard the man in the doorway behind him.

It felt like he was just standing there, watching.

The water was still cold. He turned the tap off and looked around for something to dry his hands with. The place was a mess. His mum would be horrified. Although his mum would be horrified just knowing he was in there. There were more dirty dishes spread along the worktop, and newspapers and magazines stacked up on chairs, and newspaper spread across the table, and on the table there was a gun.

He looked a second time, trying to make it look like he wasn't looking.

It was definitely a gun.

He didn't call headquarters in his head this time. There was no backup. He wasn't a detective. There was a gun on the table. His chest felt very solid all of a sudden, and he more or less stopped breathing for a moment.

But, okay, there were cloths and brushes on the table next to the gun, and some kind of grease or cleaning fluid. There were boxes of cartridges. So it was sort of okay. Sort of normal, around here, more or less normal. He'd never seen a gun before but he knew people owned them. It was a shotgun, probably. It was for shooting rabbits or whatever. It was normal. He pretended he hadn't seen anything.

The man was still standing in the doorway. He asked if the oil was coming off. Deepak looked. The soap was black with it, and there were oily smears all over the sink. He told the man it was all done, and he'd have to get going. He tried shaking his hands dry. Even if there had been a towel he would have wrecked it.

He needed to get a move on. He'd be late finishing the paper round. His mum would have kittens. The man was still talking. He wanted to look at Deepak's hands. He told him to scrub them a bit harder. Deepak said it was fine, and he should probably be getting on. The man came and leaned over him and turned the tap back on.

You just need to scrub a bit harder, he said.

Deepak let the water pour over his hands, and looked through the kitchen window. It was light outside, and in the small garden a blackbird was rooting around under a bush. The search party he'd heard people talking about would probably be setting out from the visitor center around now. The girl would be found, if she was still up there on the hill. He wondered what it might have been like, spending the night up there. He wondered what she might have been hiding from. If that was what had happened.

He had met her, back in the summer. They all had. She'd been all right. He hadn't told his parents this, before, but now he thought he probably should. The police had said any little detail might help.

He wanted to go home and tell them now.

The water poured over his hands, and he kept scrubbing, and the man said he was nearly done.

He hoped his bike would be okay. He hadn't locked it or anything.

4: Graham

The important thing to remember, Graham always said afterwards, was that no one had actually died.

There were questions to answer, and lessons would be learned; of that there was no doubt. But those people who had made so much fuss about what had happened would do well to bear in mind the lack of fatalities.

Vijay wasn't immediately reassured by this. Shouldn't they have taken more precautions, he said; shouldn't they have cut the walk short as soon as the weather turned?

Everyone had signed consent forms, Graham reminded him. They knew what they were letting themselves in for.

Graham and Vijay had led these walks for several years without incident. This was another overlooked factor in the subsequent hullabaloo: the number of miles they'd covered without mishap of any kind. In fact, if you were to calculate the average length of walk, and the average number of walkers, you'd be talking about many thousands of miles of incident-free walking.

But, no. People preferred to accentuate the negative.

The buck stopped with Graham, unfortunately. He was employed by the Park Authority, and had completed the risk assessment. He had written up the incident report. Vijay had been there in a strictly voluntary capacity, and his liability was limited. Not that there was anything to be liable for, as Graham was able to make clear.

They operated well as a team, but it would be fair to say that Vijay was the more cautious of the two, the more inclined to worry. This perhaps had to do with his day job, as an insurance broker. Plenty of the old crunching numbers, double-checking the paperwork. Graham had always been more of a seat-of-the-pants man, by contrast; stick a finger in the air and see which way the wind's blowing was his approach.

Not that Vijay wasn't an outdoorsman. Far from it. He was a very keen walker. He had all the gear. This was one of their few differences. Graham was of the opinion that good shoes were all that counted; everything else was just the leisure industries taking you for a ride. Whereas Vijay always had the latest piece of gear, the technical fabrics and spring-heeled shoes and GPS what-have-yous. And walking poles. They'd had some lively discussions about the need for walking poles. Vijay had a lot to say about hip alignment and cartilage impact. Graham's point of view tended towards the fact that they weren't in the ruddy Himalayas.

*

The walk that day was a butterfly safari, which was always popular. A full seventeen people turned up, including a party of Girl Guides and their leader. The forecast was good, and the weather when they set off from the visitor center was still and fair.

The first part of the walk was straightforward enough, although as always there were those who struggled. The climb up the track towards Black Bull Rocks could be thought steepish if you weren't used to it, and the Girl Guides were carrying a full set of camping gear each, for some reason. They swayed as they walked, with the weight. The chatter and giggles soon died down, and they were left with the tapping of Vijay's walking poles. The ground was hard—it had been dry for weeks, after a month of heavy rains, which turned out to be relevant, later—and the dust kicked up around their boots.

Graham took the opportunity to tell the group a little more about where they'd be walking and which species they might see. The heather beds they would pass were good feeding grounds for common blues and small coppers, and the knapweeds around the old mine workings were regular haunts for painted ladies. He told them a little about the industrial heritage: mines, quarries, the modern cement works. It's important not to see this as any kind of unspoiled, "natural" environment, he said. There's plenty of nature here, but there's nothing natural about the landscape.

As always, people's attention started to drift.

They came over the top of the hill and set out along the ridge, and the noise level rose again. The Girl Guides lagged behind quite early on, stooping under their heavy loads.

Graham and Vijay fell into conversation, which Graham didn't always welcome. Vijay sometimes took an excessive interest in Graham's personal life. There was a colleague he'd been working closely with, and Vijay had found it hard to believe there was no romantic involvement. There had been a lot of speculation, mostly wide of the mark. But he was less interested in it that day, thankfully. He had a new pair of walking trousers and was keen to discuss them. Graham said he didn't need to know about the wicking properties, and had no interest at all in the problem of chafing. He was a little sharp, perhaps, and Vijay took the lead for a while, opening up quite a distance between them. The two of them had these fallings-out from time to time, but they never lasted long.

They'd been crossing the flat stretch of moor-top known as Black Bull Bottoms, beyond Black Bull Rocks. It was always a bit of a slog. There was no real path as such, just a rutted cutting through the peat, waymarked by piles of gritstone slabs every few hundred yards. Vijay had stretched the distance between them to two waymarks when the hazy heat of the afternoon thickened quite suddenly to a rolling milky mist. Graham waited for the party to regroup. Once they'd caught up he did a quick headcount and carried on, asking the group to remain within sight. He had to slow his pace considerably, and it took longer than might have been hoped to reach the fence line, where Vijay was waiting for them with news of an Essex skipper that had only just moved on. Graham hadn't seen an Essex skipper up here for two years, and asked Vijay if it was a confirmed sighting.

Confirmed in what way, do you mean? Vijay asked.
Confirmed as in you're confident of the identification, Graham said.
Vijay looked at him steadily. Yes, Graham, that's confirmed, he said.

At this point it became clear that the party of Girl Guides was one short. There was quite a flurry of reaction. The Guide leader was not as calm as could have been hoped, and the other girls became hysterical. One of them went running off into the mist, and had to be caught and brought back.

Later it was realized that the girl had already been missing when Graham had done his first headcount. He may have skated over this fact in the incident report. It didn't seem important, in the run of things.

One of the positives that Graham chose to take from the events of that day was the calm and methodical way in which he and Vijay responded to the crisis. Vijay led the rest of the group down to the road to contact Mountain Rescue, while Graham and some of the other adults retraced their steps.

They fanned out on either side of the track, keeping within sight of one another, and called the girl's name at regular intervals. Graham's assumption was that she'd simply lagged behind and drifted away from the route. It seemed unlikely that she could have got far, with the weight she was carrying. But the visibility was still very poor. It was hard walking, away from the track. There were unexpected ditches and holes, and despite the dry period there were still areas of sodden ground which could suck a boot right off. In the mist the girl's name sounded muffled and thin. Graham could hear little more than his own footsteps, and his ragged breathing.

It was important not to panic.

He heard a whistle, and told the others to stop. The silence was lengthy and the mist seemed to thicken while they waited.

He heard the whistle again. They all did, and the Guide leader called the girl's name.

When they found her it wasn't where Graham would have expected. As it was, they walked straight past her twice, calling her name and pausing to listen again, and by the time they got to her she was in some distress.

Graham left the Guide leader with her for reassurance, and went to fetch help. Keep talking to her, he said; keep her awake. It was pleasing how easily he remembered the material from his training course. He made swift progress to the fence line, and then down to the road, where Vijay had already made the necessary calls.

*

When the Mountain Rescue people arrived they were brisk. They had all manner of equipment with them and they moved quickly up the hill. The Jackson boys were among them. Graham considered himself fit but he had trouble keeping up. They asked questions about the location and condition of the casualty. They expressed surprise that he had brought a group across the top in this weather, and he said it had been clear when they'd set out. It's always clear when you set out, Will Jackson said.

Graham felt the sharpness was uncalled for, but he let it go. It doesn't matter how much training or experience you have; if people have lived here longer they always think they know better. And no one had lived here longer than the Jackson family.

He led them along the path. After ten minutes they saw the torchlight he'd asked the Guide leader to flash, and they tacked off across the heather. Graham warned them to watch their step. One of them rather sarcastically thanked him for the advice. Graham took umbrage at the sarcasm, and perhaps this was why he hadn't yet explained the danger when the team leader came very close to falling twenty feet into the sinkhole where the girl was lying. One of his colleagues more or less pulled him back out of thin air.

Graham was no geologist, but it seemed that the prolonged dry spell, following months of rain, had caused a sort of rupture between different layers of peat, those layers shifting and opening up a deep crevasse, hidden by the tussocks of bog grass. The girl had wandered away from the main path and simply stepped straight into the hole. She didn't appear to be injured. It seemed likely that her backpack had absorbed some of the fall.

It was never clear, later, how long she'd been down there when they found her. It was believed she'd lost consciousness for a time, coming around in the pitch dark on a bed of soft wet peat. If she hadn't had the presence of mind to start blowing the emergency whistle it was hard to believe they would have found her at all. She would have still been down there now.

The mist started to clear, the sun burning suddenly through the last of it and the views opening up all around them. Graham was reminded why he loved walking in this landscape so much. The flat heather moorland was featureless to the untrained eye, but in fact was teeming with detail: the bilberries and bog grasses, the mosses and moths and butterflies, the birds nesting in scoops and scrapes, the bog water shining in the late-afternoon sun. The warmth was rising from the ground already, the sky a rich blue above the reservoirs in the distance. A hundred yards away, a mountain hare broke from cover and thundered across the heather.

The team hauled the girl back up to the surface on a stretcher, and as she came into the sharp light of the afternoon she squinted suddenly against the glare.

The first-aiders gathered around her, checking her condition before the long trek down the hill. Graham watched them get on with their work.

Welcome back, he said.

5: Liam

If he'd known the day was going to end with blood and fire, Liam would probably have got up earlier.

As it was, he'd stayed in bed until after lunch, and only joined the others later in the afternoon. They'd gone down to the swings by the edge of the cricket field, as always. It was hot and there was nothing to do. The summer holidays were always like this. James was on one of the swings, creaking it back and forth while he scuffed his feet along the ground. Liam was stretched out on the dry grass, trying to set fire to a small pyramid of sticks. There were bees buzzing fatly in the foxgloves by the wall. There were wood pigeons crashing about in the horse chestnut trees. The grounds-man was mowing the outfield, and the mower kept cutting out.

Then the girls turned up.

Liam saw James spit on one of his sneakers and rub at a grass stain. Deepak was doing something discreet to his hair. They were all pretending they hadn't noticed the girls.

One of the girls was Sophie, but the other one was new. They were walking all the way around the edge of the field, behind the pavilion and past the line of hawthorn trees at the top of the bank that dropped down to the river.

Sophie Hunter was in their year at school. She lived in a big house on the edge of the village. There were barns and stables and some holiday lets, as well as the actual house. The actual house had five bathrooms; Liam had counted them once. There weren't even five people living there. It was pure madness.

They'd known Sophie all their lives, but lately she'd been ignoring them. She'd started wearing makeup on the school bus sometimes, and either her skirts had got shorter or her legs had got longer. Not that any of them had mentioned it, or even really noticed.

Why she was heading their way now was almost as interesting a question as who the other girl might be.

Liam's skin was starting to itch from lying on the dry grass, but it was too late to move.

What's up, doughnuts? Sophie said.

There'd been a reason she'd started calling them this, once. Now it had just stuck.

They all muttered hello, and looked like they were waiting for the girls to move on. Sophie introduced the other girl: Becky. Becky Shaw. She was staying in one of the barn conversions, apparently, and her family was around for a fortnight.

We were thinking about going swimming, Sophie said.

The boys nodded.

At the flooded quarry, in the woods, Becky said. I found a gap in the fence yesterday.

Sweet, James said, standing up. That was all it took to make a decision. We'll go and get our stuff.

Liam gave up trying to light the fire, and got to his feet. Becky held out her hand to help him up. Her hand felt small but she was strong. He nodded thanks, ignoring the way James and Deepak were looking at him.

What's that? Becky asked, pointing to a buzzard that had been quartering overhead for a while.

Golden eagle, said James.

Millennium Falcon, Liam said.

*

They met up at the market square about ten minutes later and walked towards the meadow behind Top Lane. The heat coming off the road was making Liam dizzy. The girls were ignoring them and talking to each other.

The grass in the meadow was long but there was a flattened path running up the side. Thompson had brought his herd in for grazing and there was a deep smell of cowpat. And flies, lurching up from the ground in fat lazy clouds. They heard a pair of gunshots from high up on the moor.

None of them had actually swum in the quarry before. That was something the older teenagers did. It had been fenced off for years, and there were warning signs about the danger. People talked about how deep the water was, and how cold. People said it would be impossible to find your body if you drowned.

People said a lot of things.

This wasn't something they were going to discuss, Liam realized. They were going to walk up through the meadow, onto the moor, and then down into the woods to the quarry. They were going to find the gap in the fence and jump in, never mind how deep or how cold the water might be. It had just been decided.

They heard another pair of gunshots, and a baggy flock of crows lifted from the trees up ahead, spreading out in a line towards the church and the river.

It was hard work getting up the hill. The air felt close, and when they climbed the stile out of the meadow and onto the moor there was a heat haze shimmering over the heather. Liam wanted to offer his hand to Becky as she climbed over the stile, but James had got there first. He wasn't that bothered anyway. He waited. Beside the fence line running towards the ridge, he saw a scarecrow that hadn't been there before.

The others had seen it too, and stopped. It looked like it was holding a shotgun.

Liam wondered where Becky was from, and whether she'd seen anyone with a gun before. She had a look on her face as though she might not have done.

It wasn't a scarecrow. It was Clive, the man who ran the allotments and did pest control. He raised the gun in their direction. It was obviously meant as a joke. Becky screamed and ran towards the woods, and the others ran with her. Liam started to run but soon slowed to a walk. He knew where they were going.

*

It was cooler in the woods but the air felt dry. Sticks cracked beneath his feet as he walked. When he caught up with the others, they were looking for the gap in the fence. You couldn't see the water in the quarry from where they were standing, but there was a brightness through the bushes that Liam knew was the sunlight reflecting back from the hard surface.

The others looked at him when he joined them. Becky asked if he'd stopped for some snacks, and the others laughed. Sophie said something about an earthquake.

There were these jokes, sometimes. It went around in turns and you were supposed to just laugh it off. But sometimes.

The girls went a short distance away to get changed. The boys couldn't see them but they could still hear their voices. There were other sounds which might have been the rustle of their clothes.

The boys looked at one another. They'd grown up swimming to-gether, down at the river, but something felt different. It wasn't only the fact of being at the quarry. James told them not to be wimps and started stripping off. He already had his swimmers on under his jeans. Liam hadn't thought of that.

When the girls came back they all squeezed through the gap in the fence and followed a narrow trail through the bushes to the edge of the quarry.

James threw a stone and they watched it fall. It took forever, and they could barely hear the splash. When it landed a heron took off from the rocks at the side, hoisting itself into the air one flap at a time.

Do you think there are fish down there? Deepak asked. How would fish get in there, though?

There's a gap in the fence, James said.

Becky asked if they dared her to jump.

They did.

She jumped.

Liam couldn't believe it.

She jumped out and upward, and she seemed to be held in midair for a moment. The sun shone all over her, and everyone held their breath. Then she started to fall.

Her hair rose up above her. There was silence. She didn't scream until just before she hit the water, and then her scream was drowned out by the splash. She hit the water hard.

It took her a while to come back to the surface. The ripples in the water faded, and the water was flat and still, and the air was quiet again, and she still didn't come back up. Liam thought, later, that she'd probably stayed down there longer on purpose, just to mess with their heads. She seemed like someone who would find it funny to just hide out somewhere and watch people looking for her.

When she resurfaced, her screaming laughter echoing off the jagged walls of the quarry, everyone else jumped in.

Except for Liam. He wasn't a great swimmer, and he didn't want to hear any jokes about the size of the splash he would make.

They shouted at him to jump in, and he didn't. They couldn't force him.

After a while he turned away and started to make a fire. They'd probably be cold when they got out, despite the weather.

By the time they'd all climbed the steep path up from the water the fire was going well. It was crackling and there were sparks spinning up through the trees. Becky seemed impressed. She dropped her towel and started marching around the flames. Everyone joined in. They were stamping their feet. They were making whooping noises, and then they were all standing around Liam.

It happened quickly.

Becky put her hand on Liam's shoulder and started smearing dirt on his face.

The quarry god is angry with you, she said. She was smiling, as though it were a game. We'll have to make a sacrifice, she said. The others smeared dirt all over him. Their hands felt cold on his skin.

It was kid stuff. Childish. But he went along with it.

They made him stand against the fence, and tied his hands together.

Becky started making up a chant.

Something about the coward who would not jump. Something about the wrath of the water, the wrath of the gods.

It sounded like something she'd seen in a film. The others thought it was funny. They joined in.

She got an apple from her bag and put it in his mouth. She made the others hit him with branches to get rid of the curse. She told Liam they would only pretend. She spoke softly. She told him it was only a game. The others went along with it. Some of them were hitting a bit harder than just pretend.

Becky started saying: squeal like a pig, squeal. Liam thought that was taking it too far.

She pulled his swimmers down, and someone hit him really hard. Too hard.

Squeal like a pig. Oink, oink.

It was more than just jokes by then. It was out of hand. Liam tried to move away from the fence, but Becky didn't want to stop the game. He had to push her off. James was there as well, and Liam couldn't tell if James was helping him or helping Becky. He got his hands untied, and pushed them both off, and ran.

He could hear them running after him.

They probably thought it was still a game but Liam wasn't laughing anymore.

He had to pull his swimmers up as he ran. He ran quickly. It was downhill so it was easy to get the speed up. He must have run through some brambles, because when he looked down he thought he could see blood. He could hear the others shrieking and whooping behind him. They were running fast, but they didn't seem to be running as fast as he was. He didn't know what they thought they would do, if they caught him. He'd almost got down to the road at the edge of the woods when he turned and saw Becky close behind him, closer than the others. She had a wild look in her eyes. He slowed down until he could feel the gasp of her breath on his neck.

6: Claire

The screaming came from the woods behind the house.

Claire was just getting out of the shower when she heard it: a single long scream which ended abruptly. The window was open to let out the steam, and she leaned out for a look.

She couldn't see anything, of course. The air above the woods was dusty and still, and the sun was in her eyes. A pair of crows were circling. It was hard to tell if it had been a real scream or just kids mucking about. But she didn't dwell on it. It wasn't unusual to hear something going off in the woods. That time of year, with the long evenings and the kids off school, there would be all sorts happening sometimes.

It might have only been a fox in any case.

She went through to the bedroom to choose a dress.

They'd booked a table for dinner. It was their first night out in a long while, and Claire wanted to make an effort. Will's mother, Maisie, had already come round to babysit, and Claire was taking her time. She'd poured the first glass of wine. She could hear Maisie reading bedtime stories to Tom, and Tom asking for more than he knew he was allowed. Maisie was a soft touch with him but she didn't really mind. There was no rush. Will had been called out on a Mountain Rescue job, somewhere up near Black Bull Rocks, and had said he might be late.

She picked out a Chinese-looking print dress with a high button-up collar. Black, with flowers and dragons. Not quite silk but something pretending towards it. Will had liked it when she'd worn it before, a year or so previously. He'd said he liked the way it was high at the top but short at the bottom. Fashion wasn't really his thing. It was nice that he'd noticed.

She had to wriggle her way in, but it still just about fitted. She heard Maisie saying good night and squeezing Tom's door closed, and there was a long pause before her footsteps went slowly down the stairs. She checked the dress in the mirror, tugging out some adjustments and turning from side to side. She topped up her glass. She could hear Maisie moving around in the kitchen, fussing with dishes and pans. That woman. She'd say she was only wanting to help but it felt like interfering. Four sons and a husband, and she'd spent most of her life mothering them all. She wasn't going to stop now just because Will had left home.

Claire plugged the straighteners in, and started on her hair.

*

She waited until she heard Will come in before she went downstairs, glass in hand. The sound of her high heels on the wooden stairs should have been enough to make him turn his head. But when she came into the kitchen it was Maisie who looked her up and down. It made her feel like a teenager who'd been at her mum's makeup table.

I thought you were just going out for a nice quiet dinner? she said.

Claire smiled and nodded. She could see from Will's face that he'd forgotten they were going out at all. He was filthy. Maisie had already put a pot of tea in front of him.

Did it go okay? Claire asked. He nodded.

He's been twenty feet down in a sinkhole, Maisie said. Ropes and all sorts. Girl Guide fell through. They had to stretcher her out.

State of you, though, Claire said.

Peat stains like a bugger, Will said.

Looks like you've been at the fake tan, she told him.

I'll jump in the shower, he said, without moving. He made it sound like going out was going to be just another chore. Maisie smiled.

I'll go and check on Tom, Claire said.

*

In his bedroom Tom was sleeping fiercely, with the cover flung off and his pajama top pulled up to his chin, one fist laid over his eyes against the light. It didn't seem long since they'd moved him out of the cot, but he was already close to outgrowing the toddler bed. As she watched, his feet shook suddenly and he turned over. She remembered all the nights she'd spent in here with him, willing him to sleep. It had been so exhausting. They'd been so young. They hadn't been ready for it. She wasn't sure they were ready yet.

When she went through to their room, Will was sitting on the bed with a magazine. He hadn't even got in the shower. She told him the table was booked, and they were running late.

He told her it was a nice dress she was wearing. Which was something at least. He asked if it was new.

That was the problem, right there.

No, she told him, it wasn't new. He'd seen her in it before. She'd worn it to Matty Fincher's barbecue the previous summer, didn't he remember?

Maybe, he said. Remember you looking good that night. Just don't remember that dress exactly.

Well, I reckon Matty Fincher does, she told him.

She bent down to pick some clothes off the floor. She knew how that dress rode up. It was too short. But there was no response from Will. Nothing. She told him Matty Fincher hadn't been able to keep his eyes off her all evening, that he'd kept finding excuses to talk to her. Even put his hand on me at one point, she said, watching him.

Yeah, Will said. That's Matty Fincher for you.

There was shouting again from the woods, farther away. Another scream. She glanced across the landing and through the bathroom window. It looked like there was smoke going up from the direction of the flooded quarry. Who knew what was going off.

She turned in front of the mirror and thought she saw a ladder in her stocking, high on the back of her right leg. She made a show of swearing, watching Will from the corner of her eye. After a long pause he asked her what was up.

Ladder, she told him. She lifted the hem of her dress a little. Just there, she said.

She saw him looking, for a moment, and she saw him thinking about it. Then he turned back to his magazine. He sighed.

Listen, he said. I'm sorry. It's been a right day. I'm too tired now. You go out without me. Go for a drink with Donna or someone. Don't mind me. You're all dressed up now.

It was the sigh that did it. She didn't even look at Maisie on her way out of the house, and she gave neither of them the satisfaction of slamming the door.

*

Donna was surprised to see her. It had been a while since they'd been out together. But she looked at Claire's getup and said to give her five minutes to get ready. That's what friends do. Claire would do the same for Donna, if she could find someone to look after Tom. She went into the kitchen, and that big wet dog of theirs would have jumped up and ruined her dress if Donna's brother, Jack, hadn't grabbed it by the collar and held it close.

Don't mind him, he said. Only being friendly. Claire smiled, smoothing down the front of her dress. Donna's brother didn't go anywhere.

Something about Jack made her self-conscious. He looked older than she'd remembered. He must have been seventeen or eighteen. He'd grown quickly. The dog was pulling away from him, and she could see it was taking some strength to hold it back.

They could hear Donna moving around upstairs, her wardrobe door banging open and shut.

Jack was looking at her the way Will had always done when they first got together. This was the age they'd been. He'd had the same clumsy way of making his feelings clear. She felt exposed, suddenly. She pulled at the hem of her dress. It really was too short.

She asked how school was going.

I'm not in school, he told her. He was grinning. He looked pleased with himself. I left a couple of years back. I'm all grown up.

The dog had relaxed a little, and he was standing straighter. He was tall. She certainly felt noticed now.

I'd say so, she said. You are all grown up, aren't you?

She watched him blush. This was still her favorite thing: when they came across all cocky but you could still make them blush.

He took the dog out of the room, and when she turned to pour a glass of water at the sink she felt him come back and stand very close behind her. She pretended not to notice. He was standing about as close as he could without touching her. She could feel his breath on the back of her neck, quickening.

You all right there? she asked.

He reached around, took the glass out of her hand, and drank.

Thirsty, he said.

She turned to face him. She had to press back hard against the sink to make sure she wasn't touching him. She looked up into his eyes, frowning slightly, wanting to know what he wanted.

He was just waiting, it seemed. He put the glass down on the counter next to her, and his hands hovered.

She shook her head, very slightly, but she kept looking and she didn't move.

*

She could leave Will.
That was something that could happen.
She could have this feeling again, or something like it. This anticipation.
The taste of it.
She was too young to have given these things up.
Will was too young to have given these things up.
She'd be doing them both a favor.
There were possibilities.

*

Donna came clattering down the stairs and started to ask Claire where they were heading. Jack had already moved away by the time Donna came into the room, but Donna still stopped what she was saying and looked at the two of them.

Claire smiled, innocently.

Jack gave Claire a look which she took to mean this would be continued. She ignored him, and followed Donna out to the car.

As they got in there was an awkward silence. Claire laughed.

You're not thinking? We didn't—what?

You just better bloody not, was all Donna said.

We didn't! Claire said, trying to laugh it off.

So many reasons why not, Donna said. Jesus, what's wrong with you?

Claire told her again that nothing had happened, and asked what Donna was even thinking, and she could tell that Donna didn't believe her by the way she accelerated through the village and down the road towards Cardwell.

When they came down the hill past the woods, a group of kids suddenly burst out onto the road. Donna had to brake sharply and swerve over to the other side.

They only stopped for a moment, but Claire recognized James Broad, and his friend Deepak, and the older Hunter girl, Sophie. Teenagers, although they looked younger because they were all in their swimsuits. The Hooper boy was there as well. She knew them all from around the village. Their hair was wet and they were laughing. Who knew what madness they'd been up to. The Hooper boy was smeared with mud, and looked like he'd been bleeding. He wasn't laughing. There was another girl there who Claire didn't recognize. Donna gave them all a furious stare through the window, and drove on. They didn't say anything about it. They'd both grown up in the village, with nothing much to do, and they both knew about the sort of things that get done to pass the time. Those long summers, with no way out. Seeing the same faces day after day. You'd feel trapped. Sometimes you'd break things just to see what would happen.

7: Clive

The gun was out on the table when the police came into the house, which was awkward.

The younger policeman in particular hesitated as the two of them came into the kitchen, and glanced at his colleague.

You'll not mind this being out? Clive asked, moving the cleaning rods and brushes aside.

As a matter of fact, sir, it's the gun we wanted to talk to you about.

Clive put the kettle on.

*

He wasn't a shooting enthusiast. He'd be suspicious of anyone who would describe themselves as an enthusiast. A gun is simply a tool for a job. A necessary job, sometimes. But there's no call for getting enthusiastic about it. That would be something else altogether.

It's a very effective tool, as it happens. A few hundred years ago, someone in Clive's shoes would have been out with traps and snares. You couldn't say the snare was a tidy way of going about things. It was a slow way to die. There were accounts of some creatures chewing their own leg off to get loose of a snare. But with a gun, they didn't even know what was coming. It was just: tock. Done. None the wiser.

Clive kept an allotment, and had done for years. One of the jobs on an allotment was keeping the weeds under control. He wasn't a puritan about it. Some people had a love of bare soil that was hard to fathom. There was no need to be obsessed. It was only necessary to keep enough of the weeds under control so as to give what you wanted to thrive a head start. That was all.

The shooting jobs Clive carried out were a manner of weeding, was the way he saw it. If there were too many rabbits on an al-lotment, none of the crops would get started. Too many crows on the moors, the grouse wouldn't breed. It was only a question of balance. Happened the shotgun was a good tool for restoring balance.

Most of the shooting he did was contract work. Rabbits, pigeons, crows; foxes from time to time. And a few of the more difficult predators, on the game estates. He called it contract work, but mostly it was a case of cash and a handshake. He took no pleasure in it, but there was a certain satisfaction in doing the job well. He avoided busy times, but if people saw him they had no need to be surprised. They still were, though, sometimes. Especially some of the newer residents.

There had been the incident with the paperboy, for example. This was what the police officers wanted to talk about, as it turned out. They called it an incident; Clive wouldn't have used that term. The lad came into the house to wash his hands, and he left again. That was all.

The gun had been out on the table on that occasion as well. He'd been cleaning it. He was a responsible gun owner, it's what he did. But it may have given the lad a start.

Just for the record, the older policeman said: why was the boy in your house?

The lad had a spot of bother with his bicycle, Clive told them. Just out the front there. So he'd gone and offered some help, and once it was sorted the lad's hands were mucky with bike oil. So he naturally enough told him to get inside and get scrubbed up.

Naturally enough, sir, the older policeman said.

They had a way of saying "sir," some of them. Clive didn't appreciate it.

Was there a problem with that? Clive asked. Should he have done a criminal-records check first, was that what they were saying? Did he want to have risk-assessed the soap?

The police didn't always have a sense of humor. They wanted more details. How long was the boy in the house? Did he only go into the kitchen? Did he say anything about the gun?

Clive was very clear about that. The lad had never mentioned the gun. Clive had noticed him looking at it, and wondered if it might have alarmed him. He wasn't from around these parts. But he hadn't said a word, which was why Clive had thought no more about it. Until these two turned up with their questions.

But why had the lad involved the police? Clive asked. He would have been happy to talk to the boy's parents, and explain about his gun-safety procedures; reassure them. It didn't seem like a police matter.

The two of them looked at each other.

I imagine there's a heightened sensitivity, sir, the younger one said. Given current circumstances.

They were talking about the missing girl, of course. No one was talking about anything but, it seemed. It was tragic for the parents, fair enough, but Clive didn't entirely see why it had to be tragic for everyone else. They all had their own crosses to bear.

Could we ask you, the older one said, just as a matter of routine: where were you exactly, on the afternoon and evening in question?

*

He'd been at home all day, on the afternoon in question. Went to bed early with a hot-water bottle. No one had any business being out on the hills, on a night like that. It got cold quick up there, if you weren't paying attention. Beautiful, mind. The type of cold it got, that time of year. Ice on everything. All the growth stripped off. You could see the bones of the place. Frost deep down in the soil, breaking it up. Killed off the pests. It was a cleansing, of sorts. Clive liked to see a proper cold spell.

He wasn't one of those wandered-lonely-as-a-cloud types. He was a practical man. He'd worked his whole career for the water company, starting way back when some of the reservoirs were still being built, helping keep them in operation all those years. Folk had no idea how much was involved. Out of sight, most of it. Sluices and spillways. Hydraulics. Twenty-four-hour job keeping the system in balance.

But the whole landscape was a working environment. Everything had its place. Everything had its job to do. No point being sentimental about it. But he could appreciate seeing a thing work well, and understanding how it worked. The engineer in him could appreciate that.

Same on the allotments, in the spring, all the new shoots coming up, the pea shoots winding around anything close at hand. It was just cracking good design. Evolution, call it what you like. Was a pleasure to see it.

Or take the rabbits. Some people might assume that shooting the arse out of them indicated a certain disrespect on his part. Not at all. They were wonderful creatures to look at. When you peeled the skin off and saw how the muscles were knit together, the joints, the blood vessels. Nothing wasted. A little masterpiece. Same with the crows: the way the wingspan stitched into the body, the whole structure just built for flight, right down to the hollow bones. We are well made, was the point of it. Fearfully and wonderfully made, as it said in the Bible.

He'd always been struck by the truth of that when he used to go swimming up at the reservoirs. Years ago. When he first started working up there. Him and another lad would go off swimming after hours, in the summer. If you looked at the span of muscle and bone across the shoulders of a strong swimmer, there was something almost winglike about it. Like wings folded away under the skin there. If he'd been an artist he would have liked to draw it. Study it. The way bodies are slotted together. The engineering of it, to use that term again. The way muscles and bones move beneath the skin. Even the technology of skin itself, the effective waterproofing of it. The way sweat passes out of it but water never gets in. The way water just beads up on the surface and runs down, follows the contours. And the cooling mechanism: the blood flushing to the surface when the body gets overheated. Ingenious, really. A marvelous sight.

*

The police had more questions. Where were you the day after the girl went missing? Did you see anything that day, or the following day? Were you out walking, perhaps, did you see anything out of the ordinary?

They weren't particularly imaginative questions, in Clive's opinion. They were easily answered.

They wanted to know more about the gun, of course. He showed them his license, and the certificates. He showed them the locker it was kept in. They asked why the gun hadn't been in the locker when the lad came into the house.

He'd been cleaning it, he told them. He'd not been expecting company.

The pair of them seemed to run out of steam. Clive got talking to the younger one while they filled out some paperwork. He was the more approachable of the two. Thoughtful lad. A P.C. Forshaw.

They got on to allotments. P.C. Forshaw had just taken on a plot over in Cardwell, it turned out. Clive told him the trick with allotments was making sure to put the hours in. Always plenty to do. You reach this age, he said, it gets so it's something to do with the days. Good way of using up some energy.

P.C. Forshaw saw the sense in that. He was with Clive on the rabbit problem as well. Said it was quite bad over in Cardwell.

Trouble with rabbits, Clive told him, is they breed like rabbits. This was one of his jokes. They were rotten for it, in the spring. Out of control. Hard to fathom. Some people are like that, it seemed. No self-control whatsoever. Couldn't see the point of it, himself. All that nonsense.

The younger policeman had been reminding Clive of someone, and it took him a while to think who it was. One of the lads he'd known when he first worked on the reservoirs. Not long after the war. Smart lad. Good engineer. Didn't chat too much on the job. Good swimmer as well. He wasn't around for all that long, only a few years. Would have gone back home at some point, Clive assumed. He didn't know where to. A lot of people had moved up here temporarily, when they were still building the reservoirs, Clive among them. But he'd never found a reason to leave, himself. Didn't have a family to go back to, as it were. Never fancied settling down to family life up here either. Families being a snare of a kind. Not that he'd ever seen someone chew their own leg off to get away from a family, but he'd known some who had come close. Wasn't for Clive. He liked company but he liked time to himself as well. He kept things in order at home and he liked things quiet.

He'd never done much of the swimming after that other lad had left. Couldn't find anyone who took the same liking to it.

*

The two policemen had to get going, in the end. They stood up to leave before Clive had finished talking. That happened, sometimes. More than he'd like to expect. He wasn't a talkative chap. It was just that on occasion he got into a flow.

He asked if they were all square. They said they'd be in touch if they had any further questions. Clive said perhaps they could ask the lad to pop in and say hello. So that he could clear up any concerns the boy might have, any misunderstanding. They said it would be better if he contacted the boy's parents directly.

He asked if they wanted one more cup of tea before they went, but they said they had to get on.

He turned his attention back to the gun.

8: Martin

It wasn't even a llama, for starters.

He'd had to clear up that misunderstanding more than once. People had been quick to tell the story—oh, here's a good one, did you hear about Martin and that llama? Well, the joke was on them, because it hadn't been a llama in any case.

People liked talking, in these parts. There was always a story going around, and they generally took on a life of their own. But he wanted to set this particular one straight.

He'd been thinking about getting the wife a dog.

Not a great big one. Something easy to manage. But something to keep her occupied. He thought it might cheer her up.

A butcher's dog. It made sense. He didn't know why they hadn't thought of it before.

Things had been sticky with the wife for a while. She'd been unpredictable. Both kids had left home, and the two of them were rattling around a bit. Martin found himself down at the pub more often than not, and who knew where Ruth was some nights. And then the shop was running itself into the ground, on top of everything else.

Things weren't all roses and sunshine, basically. He needed something to turn it around. He'd been thinking her birthday might be the opportunity.

This particular evening, he'd been down at the Gladstone for a quick pint with Frank, who used to work at the quarry. Frank had been going on for a while about some trip to the doctor's. Martin was nodding a lot, but not really listening.

Anyway, he said, when Frank stopped talking. I've been thinking about getting the wife a dog. For her birthday.

When's the birthday? Frank asked.

Tomorrow, Martin said.

Problem, Frank said.

Martin agreed. It was a problem.

Leave it to me, Frank said, and went off to the bar.

*

When they got outside the evening was still warm. It was the type of evening Martin could have done with just sitting out in the garden, watching the sprinkler. But Frank had talked to Tony, and Tony had made some calls, and now they were heading over to Cardwell, to talk to a man about a dog. Someone knew someone who was breeding. Had some spares to get shot of.

Martin could tell it was going to be a long night. The last time they'd got involved in a mission like this they'd come close to getting arrested. They'd been trying to get rid of some scrap. It hadn't gone to plan.

Frank drove. He always drove fast, although his car didn't seem built for it. The lanes were narrow and the verges overgrown, and the weeds whipped against the side of the car. The sun was starting to lower, and it flickered through the high hedges.

Frank was telling a long story about getting his appointments mixed up at the doctor's, or being sent to the wrong department, or something. Martin couldn't really hear above the noise of the engine and the air whistling through the gaps around the door. Well, that's doctors for you, he said, when it seemed like the story was finished.

They parked up in Cardwell and went to a pub called the Grapes. Martin felt on edge already. Folk didn't go over to Cardwell much. There was history. While he was getting the round in, Frank told the barman they were looking for a man by the name of Rake.

That was standard.

It was usually clear which way things were headed when there were folk involved with names like Rake.

The barman said he knew no one with that name.

Frank stood his ground.

Said he'd been told to meet Rake there. Said he was happy to wait.

The barman said he could wait all he liked, he still wouldn't know anyone called Rake.

They sat in the corner and waited. The place was basically empty, but there was some kind of fuss going on in the pool room. Two women arguing, it sounded like. Martin wasn't sure, but he thought one of them sounded like Will Jackson's girlfriend. That would be a turnup. He was just about to mention it to Frank when a young lad came over to their table, nodded, and sat down. He dropped a pouch of tobacco and some papers on the table, and started rolling a cigarette.

You're looking for Rake? he said, talking in a low mutter.

Correct, they told him.

This one's after a dog for his wife, Frank said, nodding towards Martin.

The lad thought that was hilarious for some reason. Told them he could get a puppy within the hour. Your man Rake's desperate to get shot of them, he said. It was surprising what you could come by, around here, if you found the right person to ask.

So then it was back in the car, following this lad, hurtling down the narrow lanes, trying to hear what Frank was saying about X-rays and waiting times while also trying to work out where they were headed. The sun was nearly down, and when they came through the woods the road was suddenly dark.

*

They were somewhere on the far side of the reservoirs when they got out of the car.

It wasn't much of a place. Looked like a scrapyard of sorts. Corrugated-iron fencing. Lots of chains and padlocks, warning signs. Inside, there were sheds and kennels, a lot of mud, and three dogs roaming around on long chains, barking. The lad from the pub went and knocked on a caravan at the far end.

Martin gave Frank a look. He didn't like the way this was going.

The lad came back and said Rake was all out of puppies but Woods might be able to help.

Well, now. Woods was a name you didn't want to hear at that time of night, in a strange part of the valley and with dogs barking all over the place. Woods was a man you wanted to avoid getting involved with, if you could help it.

But they'd come this far. Martin was out of options.

Right then, he said: let's go and see Woods.

You don't go and see Woods, the lad said. Woods comes to see you.

He said the price was going to be a hundred, and he needed half of it up front. Martin was ready to leave by then, but Frank just handed the money over.

Martin knew there was no point discussing it.

The lad said they were welcome to wait in the caravan, and left.

The dogs were still barking, and this tall lad in the doorway of the caravan was looking over at them. It was dark by then, and getting cold, so they thought: what the hell. Why not.

Rake nodded hello as they ducked through the door, and pointed to a sofa at one end of the caravan. He opened a beer, but didn't offer one to Martin or Frank. Which was fair enough. It was unlikely he'd been expecting guests. They had to move some piles of clothes and magazines before they could sit down.

It wasn't a big caravan. It had a smell of being lived in, and was a squash with the three of them in there. It was damp and stuffy, even with the door open. Rake was up to something with some pots and pans on the stove. Not cooking exactly, just sort of poking around. He was too tall to stand up straight in there, so he was stooping around the whole time. Skinny as well. A bony face, with a crooked nose.

There wasn't much in the way of conversation. Frank was trying to tell Martin something about his wedding anniversary, of all things. And then they just sat there, waiting. Rake rolled himself a cigarette, and stood there smoking it and watching them. You can put the television on if you want, he said. But they couldn't get it to work.

The whole time they were sitting there, Martin was remembering the stories he'd heard about Woods. He was trying to work out how they could leave. Frank seemed more relaxed.

Eventually they heard a car outside, and there was a sweep of headlights across the yard. Doors slammed, and the dogs started barking more loudly. Through the open door they saw a big lad come marching towards them. This was Woods, they took it.

Martin had never actually met him before, despite knowing his name all that time. The man looked like he'd been a rugby player twenty years before. He had that size but it had all gone soft. A smooth head. One of his ears was mashed. He was carrying something in a plastic bag.

He came up the steps and leaned in through the door. The whole caravan rocked. He nodded to Rake, and asked who was after the dog. Martin put his hand up, like some sort of schoolboy, and Woods dumped the bag in his lap.

All out of dogs, he said. But these are popular.

Martin looked in the bag. The smell was terrible. Whatever it was, it had a lot of dirty white hair.

Llama, Woods said. Baby llama.

Martin was not expecting that. That was nonstandard. But time was getting tight.

He lifted it out of the bag and had a good look at it. He was a butcher, not a vet, but he knew a thing or two about animals. This one was in a bad way. The eyes were all gummy and the breathing was off. Quick and shallow. And there was the smell.

He looked at Woods, and at Frank.

It's not even a bloody llama for a start, he said to Frank, quietly.

No? asked Woods. What is it, then?

It's an alpaca, is what it is, Martin told him.

If Woods was surprised, he didn't show it. Well, mate, he said; whatever it is, it's yours now. He stepped outside and started talking to the other lad.

Martin said to Frank, muttering: This is no good. This won't do the job at all. Look at the bloody state of it. It's nearly dead. What am I going to do with a dead bloody alpaca? Hide it in the garage? If my wife comes home and finds a dead alpaca in the garage, I'm going to get bloody divorced. No marriage counseling, no trial separation, I'm going to get bloody divorced. And I don't want to get divorced, Frank. I love my wife, okay?

It was the most he'd said all evening. Frank didn't reply.

Woods came back into the caravan and asked if they were all good.

Mr. Woods, Martin said. No disrespect, but this wasn't what we were looking for. It's for my wife. She really wanted a dog. I'm sorry. As though he were apologizing for not wanting to buy a half-dead alpaca.

Woods just looked at him. He repeated the price. He told Martin it was late, he was tired, and Martin was going to take the so-and-so alpaca whether he so-and-so wanted to or not.

They handed over the rest of the money. They took the alpaca and went to get in the car.

They didn't talk much on the way back. They had to wind the windows right down on account of the smell. The air rushing in was cold and sharp. When they came along the road above the reservoir the moon was shining off it.

Frank said that anyway, what he'd been trying to say earlier was that he'd finally got a new appointment sorted at the hospital, next week, for a something Martin didn't quite catch. He looked like it was important so Martin asked him to repeat it.

BIOPSY, Frank said.

Oh, right, Martin replied.

It was probably nothing. These doctors. They'd whip you in for tests at the drop of a hat. It would be nothing. You look fit as a fiddle to me, he said.

They stopped off at the reservoir car park and got rid of the alpaca.

Martin asked Frank if he had any more good ideas about the wife's birthday. Frank did not. They were quiet the rest of the way back.

9: Stephanie

She never asked for names, but she was good at remembering faces. So when she saw the two of them being interviewed on the news she recognized them immediately, even though it must have been fifteen years since they'd last met.

They'd come to see her one evening, when she was working. Or rather, the young man had come to see her. It had been arranged. The older man had driven him there.

She watched them get out of a Land Rover and cross the driveway, their boots heavy in the gravel. She was already cautious, with there being two of them. She opened the door and checked the name. The older man seemed impatient to get inside. She told him they were out of sight on this side of the house, but he didn't seem reassured.

The young man was nervous, once they got inside.

The men were often nervous, more so than they wanted to admit, but this one didn't seem to want to be there at all. She watched him while the older man, his father, told her what was required. He spoke to her as if she worked in a restaurant and he was ordering food from a menu. She didn't like his tone. He thumped his son on the back and went to wait in the car.

She led the way upstairs. The whole setup felt unsatisfactory. The boy couldn't even look at her. He was wearing a heavy jacket, and he was flushed and sweaty. She asked how old he was, and when he said eighteen it sounded like a lie. She'd be lucky if he turned out to be sixteen. She could smell beer on him, and asked how much he'd had to drink. A couple, he said, and she guessed it was more than that.

Your first time? she asked, and he nodded.
Sort of, he said. Meaning very much so, she knew.

She talked to him, first. She didn't want to do anything until he could at least look her in the eyes. She took his jacket off, as a way of letting him feel okay about being touched, and made him a cup of tea. She asked him some questions.

He'd not long left school, he told her, and was working for his father. They were hill farmers. They kept sheep. They were a big family, with three other brothers at home. He was the oldest. She asked if coming to see her had been his idea, and he shook his head. She asked if he felt okay about being there. He hesitated, and looked up at her. There was an uncertainty in his eyes; a fear of saying the wrong thing. He told her he wasn't sure, that it depended, and did she feel okay about being there?

*

She felt fine about being there.

She'd been working in the area for a couple of years by then. A friend had set her up. She was well-enough known to stay in business, but not enough that anyone talked. The men certainly didn't. They were mostly married, or had other reasons for wanting to be discreet.

She worked from a holiday cottage. There were no neighbors, and cars could be parked around the back, away from the road. Her friend kept an eye on things, and he would always be in the house if she was meeting somebody new. It was a straightforward arrangement. The money was good, and the complications few. She wasn't planning on doing it forever. She was in control. She felt more in control than the men who came to see her, many of whom seemed muddled and lonely, or resentful of her for some reason. Angry, sometimes. She'd had to call her friend through from the other room on occasion. The men were always surprised to see him; outraged, as though it were cheating in some way.

She didn't tell the young man any of this, of course. She just said she was comfortable being there. It was funny how often she had to have this conversation. All those concerned men wanting to know if she was okay, or if there was something different she could be doing with her life. And yet there they were, knocking at her door, paying her for sex. The idea of rescuing her was just another control fantasy, much the same as paying her to do something they thought she might not want to do.

I never do anything I don't want to do, she sometimes had to tell them. They seemed disappointed to hear it.

*

He'd dressed up for the occasion. He was wearing a pair of black jeans, and a checked shirt which was clean but hadn't been ironed. She imagined a household where only the mother did any ironing. His hair was thick and black, parted exactly in the center, the two fringes hanging down into his eyes. He had a workingman's body, with broad shoulders and a bowed chest, but a boy's face. There were still spots spread across it, and a rawness that made it look as though he'd shaved just before coming out. She could imagine his father explaining how he should dress, how he should proceed; as though explaining how to approach a job interview, or the best way to handle a sheep.

He kept sipping his tea before it was ready to drink, and burning his mouth, and then pretending he hadn't. There was an eagerness about him, once he began to relax. An eagerness to impress, to be thought mature, but also an eagerness to get on with it. The reluctance was gone.

She had mixed feelings about going ahead. This was why she'd started a conversation first. She understood what the father thought this was. She could imagine him pacing back and forth outside. She was reluctant to go along with this idea, of the older woman initiating a younger boy. She wasn't Mrs. bloody Robinson. He should learn about these things with a girlfriend, when the time came.

But still, beneath the nerves and the shaving rash, there was something so hopeful in the way he looked at her. She didn't want to disappoint him; and she could tell, from the way the older man had spoken, that he would have good reason not to let his father down. She took his cup of tea and set it to one side. She moved him over to the edge of the bed, and started to undress.

And she enjoyed the thrill in his eyes. Of course she did. That was part of it, sometimes. He was hurried and clumsy, once he got started. She slowed him down by making him practice unfastening her bra. This is the most useful thing you'll learn tonight, she told him. She had to put the condom on for him, and then it was over very quickly. He made no sound at all, but when she asked he said that yes, he'd enjoyed it. He'd stopped looking her in the eye again. He was ashamed, and she told him not to be.

Afterwards he seemed confused about what to do. She offered him some tissues to clean himself but he'd already pulled up his trou-

sers. She dressed, and opened the door. He said thank you, a number of times, and shook her hand. She told him to take care, and
that it was generally not the done thing to shake hands after sex.

*

His father came up into the room then. Payment had already
been taken so at first she didn't understand why he was there. He
wanted to know how things had gone. It seemed inappropriate.
She tried to keep things light and told him she didn't like to com-
promise client confidentiality. He hadn't paid her to be bloody
confidential, he said.

She kept a distance and told him she wasn't going to discuss it. He
persisted. He wanted to know if he had anything to worry about,
with his boy, if there were any problems.

He could have been talking to his vet about a wayward sheep-
dog. He had nothing to worry about, she told him. His son was
fine. She hated going along with his way of thinking, but there
was something in his manner that made her worried for the boy's
safety. She'd understood the boy's nervousness, then.

The father seemed satisfied with that. He relaxed. He took off his
jacket and started unbuckling his belt. She tried to make light of
this as well, saying that she didn't even know his name yet, but he
didn't seem in the mood for humor. He seemed—heated. She had
to tell him, quickly, that she didn't work with more than one client
in an evening. And he laughed, as though that were a joke. Usually,

repeating herself clearly and firmly was enough for someone to get the message. She folded her arms, and said she was done for the evening. You can make an appointment for another time, she told him, knowing she wouldn't take him on. He laughed again, with even less humor than the first time, and took a big step towards her.

She knew what was coming.
She called for help.
He grabbed her by the shoulder and smacked her across the face.

It wasn't a slap. He caught her with the heel of his hand, hard, and she went down to the floor with her vision slanted and her ears whistling. Her friend was in the room quickly, taking hold of the man's arm just as he lifted his belt above his head. He was hustled outside. There was more violence then, she was sure, but it happened out of earshot and she didn't ask her friend about it afterwards.

Despite what she'd worried about when she first got into the work, and despite what she thought she knew about the business as a whole, this was the closest she'd come to being in proper trouble the whole time she'd worked there. It had scared her, undoubtedly. The rage on his face had been so thorough, and had come on him so abruptly. She'd wondered what he'd done with it, later. She'd worried about the son.

They'd moved on, after that. Her friend had said it would only be sensible. Men like that, in an area like that, tended to have associates. They tended to talk. They were—territorial.

It wasn't worth waiting around to find out what might happen if he came back, was how her friend put it.

It put the wind up her for a while, but she soon recovered. She worked for a few more years, in various places. And although she occasionally remembered the young man, she would have said she'd forgotten what he looked like, until she saw him on the news.

There was a story about a missing girl, in the village near where she'd worked. The reporter was asking what people in the village felt about the girl's disappearance. His name was strapped across the bottom of the screen.

Gordon Jackson, Sheep Farmer.

He was saying they all had sympathy for the family, they couldn't believe what had happened, it was terrible, they'd all taken part in trying to find her. His father was in the background, talking to someone else, pretending to ignore the camera. She remembered him even more clearly than the son. He hardly seemed to have aged at all.

Gordon Jackson, Sheep Farmer, kept talking. His voice was deeper now, and rougher. It was shocking weather to have gone up top on the moor, he said. We could all see that. The girl should never have been up there in the first place. She had no business wandering around up there on her own.

The reporter thanked him, and he nodded, and as they cut back to the studio she saw him glance away from the camera, towards his father.

10: Donna

By the time the man came into the pub to say he was looking for his daughter, Donna had already had enough of the evening. She could have done without the drama.

The man was with Stuart Hunter. Stuart wasn't often seen in the pub, so people had fallen quiet before either of them started speaking. It was a Sunday evening, and there were only a dozen or so regulars in the small lounge bar. Donna was there with Claire, trying to get her sobered up after an evening over in Cardwell that had got out of hand.

We were expecting her back about an hour ago, the man said. She's probably just lost track of the time. I was wondering if anyone may have seen her around. She's nearly thirteen. About this tall.

He held a hand to his chest, and then seemed to reconsider, looking down and lifting his hand towards his chin.

She's got dark blond hair, he said. Collar-length.

This was the same girl who went missing the following winter. The whole evening felt like a trial run, when Donna remembered it later.

Tony's first response was that they didn't serve teenagers, so he would have noticed if she'd been in unaccompanied. He seemed to have taken offense. Tony took offense easily.

The girl's father said of course, he understood, but was it possible she'd popped in and out, was it possible she'd sat in the beer garden without coming into the bar? They were sure she hadn't gone far, he said. She was probably just wandering about and had lost track of the time. She'd done it before. They were trying to retrace her steps. She didn't know the area.

Stuart said that the girl had been out with his daughter Sophie for most of the afternoon, but that Sophie didn't know where she was now.

She does this, the man was saying. I'm sure she'll turn up. He seemed embarrassed, more than anything.

Donna tried to catch Claire's eye, but she was in another world. Lounging across her armchair like the queen of France, ignoring the coffee Donna had bought for her.

Donna went over to the bar. I think we saw her earlier, she told them. With Sophie. Down by the woods. We were on our way to Cardwell and there was a whole group of kids out on the road, near the entrance to the old quarry. There was one girl we didn't recognize. Maybe that was her?

The girl's father thanked her. Tony suggested they all go and take a look, and there was a general move towards the door, glasses left half-empty on the tables as they spilled out into the square.

Tony asked Donna what the hell they'd been doing going over to Cardwell. Fancied a change of scene, Donna told him.

In Cardwell? he said. Had a good evening, did you?

I've had a bloody excellent evening, Claire told him, in her loudest whisper; but don't tell Will.

*

Outside it was still warm, but the air was turning damp and the light was falling away. People spread out quickly through the streets, peering over walls and into back gardens and alleyways, knocking on doors.

If it weren't for Claire, Donna would probably just have slipped away home. It seemed likely the girl wouldn't have gone far. She's done this sort of thing before, the girl's father was saying. I really don't want to cause a fuss. She always turns up in the end. Donna watched him. There was something there that reminded her of her own father. He seemed embarrassed by his daughter's actions; or maybe embarrassed that he'd let her out of his sight. Her own father had lost his way with her by the time she turned ten or so. He'd kept calling her his baby girl, his baby princess, as though if he said it often enough she would never grow up.

The man had wiry dark hair that kept falling into his eyes, and a pair of black-framed glasses that he kept having to adjust.

Donna was just about to ask him about his daughter when Claire came stumbling up and grabbed her by the arm.

What are we doing again? she whispered.

We're looking for that man's daughter, Donna said. She's late home. He's worried about her.

I'm late home! Claire said. No one's worried about me.

You're a grown-up, Donna told her. Apparently.

*

Donna had thought of herself as a grown-up for a long time. Her father had drifted away from the family when she was thirteen, or maybe fourteen. It was hard to say. There'd been no definitive leaving. He just kept going away and coming back and going away, and eventually he stayed gone. Donna had grown up quickly, after that. Their mother had never really talked about it, but there'd been a gap in the household that needed filling. Her baby brother had been too young. And too male. Donna had had to look after them all for a while, until her mother got back on her feet. That had taken a few years.

And now here she was again, looking after Claire. Practically holding her up. They weren't being much use to the search. They'd stopped before they'd even got to the far side of the market square, falling behind the others. They were leaning against the wall by the bus stop, while Claire rummaged through her handbag. She was looking for her cigarettes, emptying everything out onto the wall, getting more and more agitated. She must have left them in Cardwell, she was saying, they'd have to go back. They weren't going back, Donna told her. It was late. It was time to go home.

They could hear people farther down the street, calling the girl's name.

Claire gave up. Her breathing was ragged. The contents of her handbag were spread out across the wall like some kind of tiny flea market. Donna wanted to ask her about the evening, about what had happened and about what she thought Will would think if he ever found out. She wanted to ask what Claire thought was going to happen next.

But she was too tired to have that sort of conversation. She didn't think she'd get much sense out of Claire this evening in any case.

The stone of the wall was warm against the backs of her legs. The streetlights were just starting to flicker on, but the light at the top of the moors was still pale and open. Donna could feel her irritation ebbing away.

And then her brother showed up.

Hello again, ladies, he said, a smile spreading across his face, loping long-legged down the street like an idiot spider. He was waving a pack of cigarettes. You looking for these? he asked Claire.

She shrieked, snatched them out of his hand, and kissed him. It started out as a friendly thank-you kiss, but kept going until it was something more reckless.

It was too much. After what had happened in Cardwell, it was really too much. Donna wanted to get them away from each other. She took Claire by the arm and told her it was time to get home. Claire wriggled loose and turned to look at her.

This is none of your business, she said, steadily.

It was, though. It was all of her business. This was her brother.

Will was her friend. And didn't it always end up being her business, picking up after other people?

*

Tony and the others had come full circle back to the market square when Ian Dowsett came over and asked what all the commotion was. When they told him, he said he'd seen a girl swimming at the quarry and sent her home. The girl's father described her again and Ian said yes, that sounded like her. He was insistent that he'd seen her heading back towards the village. I didn't know her from Adam, he said; but I wasn't about to walk away from her swimming in the blasted quarry. Place is a bloody hazard. They should fill it in.

Ian's views on the quarry were well known. But he reiterated them at some length.

Tony took a phone call from someone at the other end of the village. Becky had been seen sitting in the churchyard, and was being walked back up to the pub now.

The girl's father sat down suddenly on a bench, and his whole body went limp with relief.

There we go, he said. I did think she wouldn't have gone far. I'm sorry about all this, he said, aiming his apology at Tony but awkwardly trying to take in everyone else. Tony told him there was no need for apology; they were happy to help, they were glad it had turned out well.

Someone brought a whisky out from the pub and set it on the
bench next to the man. There was a feeling of people not knowing
whether to applaud, or what exactly they should do. It felt igno-
rant to just walk back into the pub and return to the conversations
that had been interrupted when he'd first appeared with Stuart
Hunter. But at the same time they didn't want to make it too obvious they were waiting to see him reunited with his daughter.

When she arrived, walking up the street with Gordon Jackson,
looking taller than people had imagined and with her hair tied
back in a damp ponytail, Donna realized she was bracing herself.
She was expecting the girl's father to be angry, or at least sharp
with her. It would seem natural for there to be irritation mixed in
with the relief. She imagined that he would feel humiliated, and
have nothing to do with that humiliation but pass it on. As she
watched, she waited for the girl to slow down, to be hesitant about
approaching him; or even perhaps to be defiant in some way that
would be new to them both.

But none of that happened. Her father stood up. The girl walked
towards him, quickly, and said she was sorry but she'd lost track
of the time. It was such a beautiful evening, she said. I was sitting
in the churchyard and there were I think they were swallows everywhere. The man was soft with the sight of her. He opened his
arms and drew her in. He had to lift his chin slightly so that she
would fit against him. Donna turned away.

*

Later, once the man and his daughter had gone off with Stuart Hunter, and everyone else had gone back into the pub, Donna managed to get Claire away from her brother and start walking her home. She was quieter now, and finally starting to sober up.

There was the noise of a loud engine from the other end of the street, and then Will was driving towards them on his quad bike. Claire groaned, and started turning away, but he drove straight up to them and reached out an arm to pull her towards him. Donna watched Claire give in. Their foreheads pressed together and they spoke softly to each other. Donna saw Claire nodding at something Will was saying, and then she climbed onto the back of the bike. She held on tight, and they drove away without saying goodbye.

Once the sound had died down the street was quiet and still and Donna just stood for a moment. Night had fallen properly by then but there was still a blue tinge to the darkness and a damp warmth in the air. There were insects humming in the hedges around her. There were bats moving deftly overhead. She'd never liked the way you only saw them from the corner of your eye. It put her on edge.

A bedroom light went out in the house across the road. She brushed her hand through the box hedge outside the butcher's shop and a scent rose into the air.

She supposed she'd have to get home.

11: Ian

When Ian Dowsett had gone up to the village to collect Irene and bring her back to the quarry, there'd been no need for explanations. She left her mop in the bucket and got straight into the car, peeling the rubber gloves from her hands.

Now then, she said; is it bad?

Well, Ian told her. It doesn't look good.

*

Ted was still under the rocks when they got back to the quarry.

Would have been a miracle if he hadn't been. The rockfall was stacked halfway up the face.

Ian could see from the way the pieces were sitting that the weight wasn't all on him. They'd have been scraping up the leftovers with a trowel, otherwise. But the way the rocks were stacked, it was going to be like bloody *Krypton Factor* to get him out safely.

It didn't look good at all. His face was the wrong color.

The men had strapped some of the rocks for lifting, but they were waiting for specialist equipment from another quarry. The equipment should have been on site, but Tony had been cutting corners.

Tony Morrison, this was. Operations manager. Health and safety had been on him. He was finished at the quarry, after this.

Irene didn't hang around. She got straight in there, and the men stood aside to let her through. Knelt herself down on the dry limestone dust next to Ted. Found his hand and held it.

She told him she had better things to be getting on with. The man managed a smile, just about.

Don't tend to see Ted smile at the best of times, so that was something.

He couldn't move his head so he was having to look at her out of the far corner of his eyes. Could see it was a strain. Everything looked a strain for him at that point. His breathing was quick, and shallow.

Who knew what had happened. Something had just slipped. People worry about all the blasting that gets done in a quarry, but it's more dangerous what happens in between times. People lower their guard. You stick high explosives in a hole, people understand about following procedures, listening out for warnings, keeping a safe distance. Whereas you start talking about things like slope stability, people stop listening. Certain amount of corner-cutting goes on. There's always a pressure to get the job done. And then some small thing goes wrong. Something geological. The temperature changes, the ground shifts, and all of a sudden you've a man lying in the dirt with a ton of rocks stacked up upon him.

*

It's not like no one knows a quarry is a dangerous place. Sometimes the wives could talk of nothing else. The men had all had the Talk at one time or another, working at the quarry. Any little bang on the head, any broken bone, they'd get the missus wanting everything to change. You're not working in that bleeding quarry anymore, tired of worrying myself sick about you. Get yourself out of there and don't go back. It's not worth it. All of that. It never happened. They all went back, in the end.

And if it wasn't the danger, the wives would get started on the noise, and the dust. This is meant to be a peaceful place to live, but there's all that blasting going off. And the state of the laundry. All that. You'd think they'd rather there was no quarry at all. Except then what would all those lads have been doing for work. And where would all the limestone come from then. The wives knew this, really. It was only when there was an accident like that one with Ted that they got themselves all riled up again.

There was none of that from Irene just then, of course. Was hardly the time. She just stayed there, kneeling beside him in the dirt, holding his hand. Flecks of dust kept settling on Ted's face, and she kept wiping them away.

It was the first time Ian had seen those two touch each other, he realized. You'd barely ever see them in the same room, most days, and if they were walking in the street Ted would always be ten feet ahead. The two of them were not known for being insepa-rable. And yet they'd always been known as a pair. They'd been married before they moved to the village, so no one had known one without the other.

Ted came from another village not far away, somewhere to the north. He'd moved around as a young man, and come this way to work in the quarry. He'd picked Irene up in a town on his travels.

It had taken her a while to adjust to village life when they'd first moved in.

One incident Ian remembered from years back, not long after they'd arrived. There was a group of them used to meet up in the pub after work, regular. One night there was a conversation about family, and someone asked what Ted's father did for work. It was innocent enough. People were curious. Irene started to answer the question for Ted, and Ted cut her right off.

Barely even spoke. Just lifted his hand. Quickly like.

Like getting ready to swat a fly.

And Irene stopped talking, just like that.

When they left there were jokes about what his father did that Ted didn't want discussing. No one mentioned the way he'd silenced her.

People didn't think that manner of thing was anyone else's business, in those days.

*

It should have been a more private moment. The two of them there like that. If they'd been in a hospital, Ian would have made himself scarce. But he was too involved in keeping the weight off Ted, keeping him comfortable until more help arrived.

The two of them were very calm, the whole time.

Not like Tony. Tony was in bits, running backwards and forwards, on the phone, shouting instructions at the men. They were still waiting for the proper lifting gear to arrive. Where's the eff-ing ambulance, he was shouting, where's the effing rig, what's the effing holdup.

He knew it was on him. Cutting corners, letting blokes get on with it without checking what they were doing. But he was hardly rectifying the situation by running around like a blue-arsed fly the way he was.

Irene just sat in the dirt next to Ted.

Holding his hand. Looking at him.

Not like this, she said. Not now.

And Ted just looking up at her. Blinking, dead slow.

Licking his lips, but he couldn't talk.

A couple of lads got a jack underneath one of the slabs at that point, and cranked it up. Trying to get the weight off his chest. It was ill-advised. There was a crunching noise, and Ted's eyes sort of rolled back in his head.

He didn't scream. But his color got worse.

*

Word spread, the way word does.

Jackson and his boys showed up, asking was there anything they could do. They had all sorts of rig on the back of the trailer. But it was specialist gear Tony was waiting for.

The ambulance arrived. Irene had to stand out of the way while they saw to him. Not much they could do while he was under the rocks. Make him comfortable. Give him oxygen. Pain relief. They managed to get a brace on his neck. Everything else had to wait.

Jesus, though. It didn't look good.

Irene got back in there beside him. Said nothing. Held his hand again.

Blood was coming out of his mouth by then. She wiped it away with a handkerchief, and tucked it back into her sleeve.

*

It had been the beginning of the end of the quarry. Tony stopped working there not long afterwards, and although no one said there was a connection it was plain there must have been. No one quite understood how he came through the investigation in one piece.

He must have been given a payoff when he left the company, because soon after that he went and took over at the Gladstone. There'd been no pub open for a few years by that point, so everyone was glad of it. Didn't ask him any questions about the money.

The quarry company closed the whole site not long after Tony left. Not because of what had happened to Ted; those companies had deaths and injuries factored into their business plans, surely. But as it turned out, that unstable face had been the last one they'd planned to work in any case.

The regeneration crowd moved in. Stripped all the machinery they could use, broke down the rest, flooded the lot. Planted a few hundred trees, put up the nesting boxes, all that type of thing. Fenced the whole place off and put up warning signs.

Ian used to go up there with Ted from time to time and watch the progress of it all. Was like watching history in reverse, slowly.

It had taken four months for Ted to get home from the hospital, and he never lost the limp. But he made it. Broke his pelvis, and most of his ribs, and there was plenty of internal bleeding. But there was no head injury and they reckoned that was what made the difference. Iron Man, they called him after that. Made him seem invincible.

Irene was known not to be impressed when he went back to work at another quarry. But she never said a word. She couldn't. Ted wouldn't have stood for it.

He turned out not to be invincible in the end. Only lasted another six years.

All the dust in the man's lungs, they reckoned. Although Ian didn't imagine that smoking forty a day would have helped much either.

*

Ian still walked past the old quarry site now. He liked to make sure the fence was in good order. It was a peaceful place to be. Not like it had been back then, with the dust and the noise and the bare blasted rock. Now it was clear blue water, trees, birdsong. The evening air beginning to cool after a long hot August day. Dragonflies zipping about above the water, no doubt. Swallows skimming low across the surface. It seemed likely there'd be some good fishing down there, if you could get to the banks. Grayling, maybe even trout. But there was no chance he'd be trying anything like that. Trouble with all the regeneration that went on at these places, it tended to disguise the dangers. You make something look pretty enough, some idiot would forget why the fence was even there.

And this one evening, again, some kid was swimming down there. Ian had seen her and stopped by the fence to call her out. He'd seen a group of them here earlier and now this one looked to have come back again on her own. Taking her chances once wasn't good enough for her. These kids had no idea. They thought it was some kind of public lido. They had no idea there were loose rock faces down there, bits of old machinery and who knew what else under the water. And brutal cold sometimes. It was no place for swimming. He waited until she'd climbed all the way out so he could give her a piece of his mind. The evening was starting to soften, and the air in the shade of the trees was cool and damp. The water had already stilled.

The girl didn't say anything to him when she got back up to the fence, but just pushed past him and marched off down the hill through the trees. Ian couldn't tell if she was embarrassed or just rude. Didn't much matter either way. Kids were either going to learn or they weren't.

12: Irene

Irene didn't tend to have visitors. Not since Ted had died.

She was sociable enough, but she liked to see people away from the house. She was so busy with her cleaning jobs that she didn't always keep on top of things at home. She was by no means slovenly but she had very high standards. It was hard to keep up. And Andrew was getting older now. He could be disruptive around the house.

But now here she was with the third visitor in a week, breezing into the kitchen before Irene had quite had the chance to say good morning.

The young lady was from social services. She told Irene the police had been in touch, and she was here to do a needs assessment, which Irene was entitled to, it would only take five or ten minutes, here was her identity card and her referral letter, thank you, could she come in, it really wouldn't take long, thank you.

She was one of those as didn't talk in sentences but just kept going, one thing after another. It made Irene feel out of breath just to listen to her. Irene had a reputation for talking herself, she knew that, but at least she gave other people a word in edgeways. This young lady had got her feet under the kitchen table before Irene had even gathered her name. She had to clear away the breakfast things and wipe the table clean before the young lady could set down her briefcase.

The whole thing was rather confusing. She'd been expecting a telephone call from either Victim Support or Crime Prevention. She hadn't been clear which, but that was what she thought the policeman had said. Not social services. She'd never had the social around in her life. But it had been hard keeping everything straight. The policeman had done a lot of talking as well, and brought a lot of paperwork with him. But at least he'd given her a chance to speak.

Forshaw, his name had been. Nice young man. Awful thing was that he'd specifically asked her *not* to tidy up before he called around. He'd even sent someone along to take photographs.

He'd been there because of the man from the water company. Who hadn't been from the water company at all. Stupid. Stupid.

The whole thing was so embarrassing. She should have known better. But the man had been so polite, and there *had* been problems with the water pressure lately, just as he said. He told her it would only be a few minutes, and it was. He was in and out, didn't make a mess, thanked her for her time. It was a few days before she realized what had happened.

It wasn't so much what she'd lost as it was the sense of intrusion. This was what she'd told P.C. Forshaw. The thought of that man prowling around, while she kept out of his way, just as he'd asked. Picking things up and putting them down again. Slipping anything as took his fancy into that big black toolbag of his. Jewelry. A little cash. That fancy laptop of Andrew's, from the school.

She'd given the policeman a description. He was a tall man, and very skinny. He'd had to duck through all the doorways. He had a narrow, bony face and a crooked nose. That was all she could say. P.C. Forshaw had said it might well be enough, and he'd let her know if there were any developments. He told her that someone from Crime Prevention would be in touch, and at the very least they would fit a chain on the door.

Things had changed. People used to leave their doors wide open, and would never have dreamed of locking them. Now there were chains, and alarms, and who knew what else. No doubt this young lady was going to persuade her to have all manner of nonsense installed. Bars on the windows. Robot guard dogs. Goodness knew. Andrew would love that. Andrew was probably in the middle of inventing a robot guard dog, come to think of it. He was very clever on the computers. Irene had no idea what he was up to most of the time.

The young lady took some forms out of her briefcase and spread them across the table, which wasn't a great start. She talked about preliminary criteria and funding brackets, budgetary constraints and possible beneficial outcomes. She had a lot to say and she said it quickly.

Andrew was there, but he didn't say anything. He was hovering in the doorway and he just watched, with that contented smile of his. Andrew said very little at the best of times. He had some educational needs.

The young lady wanted to do a tour of the house, firstly. She said she wanted to see what was what and go through her checklist: there were a number of additionals Irene and her son might be entitled to, but she had other appointments to get to, and she was in rather a hurry, so could they get started?

She was up with her clipboard before Irene had even replied. Asking questions about door handles, grab handles, stair lifts, and who knew what else. She was brisk. As they went up the stairs, she asked how Irene managed with the shopping, with getting out and about, collecting her pension, getting to the bank. Any hobbies? Did her family live locally?

She seemed to have the wrong end of the stick. Irene wasn't retired, and she didn't have a pension to collect. She was a widow, certainly, and the very word made her feel terribly old. But she was working harder than ever. She'd had to, since Ted's passing. She got some help, but the cash from her various cleaning jobs around the village was essential. And it was all cash. It got complicated otherwise. There were forms she'd have to fill in. She didn't take to forms.

In the bathroom, the young lady asked questions Irene didn't think were appropriate.

*

In the kitchen Irene started making a pot of tea. The young lady was flicking through the papers from her briefcase. She had a calculator out on the table. Andrew was back in the doorway, just watching her. He still had the contented look about him.

What day is it? he asked the young lady.

It's Sunday, isn't it? She smiled at him, and at Irene. She seemed bemused.

Of course it's Sunday, Andrew, Irene said; you know that. What sort of a question is that, now? Don't mind him, she told the young lady. He'll ask funny questions sometimes.

Oh, no problem at all, the young lady said; it's good to be sure. I forget what month it is sometimes, you know what I mean? She laughed, quickly, and took her phone out. She'd finalized the list of what they would be able to offer, she said. She just needed to call some details through to her manager.

Irene wanted to know why she couldn't just take the paperwork back to her office, and the young lady gave her a confusing explanation about preapproval. She started talking on the phone.

Andrew suddenly excused himself and went into the back garden. He could be abrupt sometimes. He knew his own mind. There was no point asking for explanation.

The young lady was arguing with her manager. That's disgraceful, Irene heard her say. There must be something we can do; these people are entitled to our help. She put a hand over the phone and apologized to Irene.

There was a problem, she explained. Something about an overspend, something about needing to reallocate funds. She talked to her manager again.

Irene heard the side gate crash open, and saw Andrew going past the window.

The young lady was nodding a lot. She told Irene that some limited funds would be available if they could get the application in by the end of the day. She would just need a few more details, she said. And a deposit.

A deposit? Irene asked.

The young lady said something about means-tested contributions. She said they would make a final assessment later and the preliminary contribution might end up being almost minimal, but she did need to get something in that day due to the quarterly allocations deadline.

Irene said she didn't know about all that.

The young lady put her phone down on the table and gave Irene a look.

Can I be honest? she said. In the professional assessment of myself, you are not currently providing your son with the support he requires. I'm not a legal expert, she said, but in the event of anything happening with your son, this interview could be taken into account. There could be ramifications.

Ramifications?

If you could cooperate with the process, she said, that would be appreciated.

Irene told her she was cooperating, but it was a lot to take in.

And of course I am sorry to rush you, the young lady said. But we should make the most of this window of opportunity. You'll be able to discuss it with your family at a later date and the deposit is of course returnable, but I do need to get it into the system today.

Well, Irene told her. If it was nothing final.

The young lady gave her a form to sign, did some more sums on her calculator, and said the deposit would be thirteen hundred pounds. She wouldn't take a check, and nor could she arrange a bank transfer. Cash was essential, she said.

Irene only hesitated for a moment, but the young lady suddenly packed her papers away and told Irene she'd rather not waste any more time; she had other clients to see, other clients who would appreciate her efforts.

Please, Irene said. I do appreciate your efforts.

She knew something was wrong, but she still found herself opening the larder and reaching for the secret place where she kept her cash. She counted it out while the young lady watched, and was embarrassed to find only nine hundred pounds.

She asked if that would suffice.

The young lady said it would be enough to get the process started. She looked very keen to be out the door all of a sudden.

Irene counted the money once more, to be on the safe side. She handed it over, and asked for a receipt.

And then Andrew came in through the front door, with Tony

from the pub. Tony had questions. The young lady tried squeezing past him, out the door.

Tony wasn't built for squeezing past. He asked some more questions.

*

It went to show, Irene thought, later. People assumed that Andrew wasn't all there, that he had no idea of the world around him. But the boy was bright enough. He just had a different manner of putting himself about. Sat there with his blank face but there's a world going on inside. Knows what's what.

He had that young lady worked out almost as soon as she walked through the door, and he knew what to do to fix it. Smart boy. Irene didn't know where he got it. He had a nose for trouble. And for keeping out of trouble. At the school, they said Irene idealized this about him. They told her not to build it up too much. Told her to accept his limits. But they didn't see him like she did.

And so when Andrew told her that the missing girl was fine, Irene believed him. He told her he knew a few things and he knew she'd come to no harm. Irene couldn't get him to say any more. He wouldn't talk to the police. He wouldn't talk to journalists. He would barely talk to her. But he'd said enough for Irene. It had put her mind at ease. The girl would have come to no harm, wherever she was.

13: Ginny

She was sitting right there,
under the tree.
The apple tree.
Eating an apple.

In the summer. Last summer. Before

the girl went missing.

Ginny thought she was imagining it at first.

The girl would have had to climb the wall
at the back of the garden. From the meadow.

It was the girl
the missing girl,
Becky Shaw.
Ginny's sure of that now.

She wasn't missing, then.

She was sitting under the tree, the
apple tree.
Eating an apple.

Scrumping, they called it once. Children don't do it now.
More likely to see them smoking
and whatever else
down at the park, by the
cricket pavilion.
Breaking windows.
This seemed—quaint.

She looked like—
this girl
she looked like—
but it may just have been a trick
of the light.

One of Ginny's moments.

She had those.
After Jacek's death. He'd died six years ago.

It may as well have been last week.
She'd see someone who looked like him, out and about,
at the market,
in the distance,
in a passing car.
And for a moment it would be
it would really be him.

It was something she'd heard about, before.
Before.
But she'd not known
she'd not been told
how uncanny it would be.
It was always someone who looked exactly like Jacek,
for that short moment
and then they were just
gone.
It could take days to shake the feeling off,
sometimes.

And this girl in the garden, under the apple tree, she looked
she looked like Laura.
Exactly like Laura.

Laura was Ginny and Jacek's daughter. She was grown now.
She'd be—
thirty-three.

And this girl was Laura

at that age
to a T.

Different clothes, of course.
But the shape of her, the way she carried herself.
It was
Laura.

Ginny remembered Laura carrying herself
like that.
The look had come into her overnight.
They'd seen the woman in the girl.
It had been sudden.
They'd seen her realizing what kind of woman she would be, and
playing with the part. Dressing up
in different poses.
They'd seen her wishing herself
out of reach.

She'd wanted away.
That had been obvious.

Ginny could remember wanting away
from her own mother
just the same.

And the cheek.
The cheek she'd started giving them, giving Jacek and Ginny.
It was hard to know where it came from.

It nearly
broke Jacek
to hear it.

It was hard
to live through. People talk about the terrible teens
it's an awful cliché but
there's truth in it, but
they didn't know how bad it would be.

It was hard
to live through. They didn't know what they were doing wrong.
They didn't know what had got into her, sometimes.
Drink, they suspected, or

worse.

The police talked about drugs, later.
And boys, no doubt. Older boys.
Laura couldn't imagine the dangers she was
getting herself into, and
they could. They could.
That was part of the problem. She just

she wouldn't believe
they were worried about her.

She'd wanted excitement, adventure. She'd wanted
nothing to do with them.

After
after everything they'd done for her, everything
they'd given her.
They resented that. Honestly. They were angry with her for that
sometimes.

But they didn't
they didn't drive her away.
They didn't.

*

It wasn't Laura
in the garden
under the apple tree. Of course it wasn't.
It was some other girl. It was Becky Shaw,
although she didn't know that then.

She was looking at Ginny with,
she wouldn't say insolence,
although some people would call it that.

It was confidence.
There was a challenge.
A way of setting the shoulders.
As if to say, what?
What's your problem, missus?
That was the face she had on her.
What's your problem?

It wasn't rude, as such. It was more,
she couldn't imagine what problem Ginny might have,
seeing her sitting in the garden like that,
under the apple tree, eating an apple.

She wanted to get a rise, and Ginny didn't give her one.
Ginny thought that might take the wind out of her sails.

She said good afternoon, and she got on with the jobs
she'd come into the garden to do.
There was blackfly all over the runner beans.

She could feel the girl watching,
the apple halfway to her mouth.
She could almost hear the air coming out of her,
she was that deflated.

It became a waiting game, after that.
Both of them waiting for the other to speak.
Well. The girl had no idea.
Ginny knew about that game.
She'd had a lot of practice.

Not that she wasn't furious.
But she didn't want to give this girl the satisfaction of seeing how
she felt.
She could see
that was what the girl wanted.

It was all very reminiscent.

She picked off the new crop of runner beans.
She wiped down the leaves and stems with a soapy cloth.
The blackfly were all over.

The girl gave in, eventually, and spoke first.

She asked if Ginny would report her.
It seemed an odd thing to ask.

She told the girl she imagined the police had better things to concern themselves with than the theft of a single apple. And she didn't know the girl's parents, so she could hardly talk to them, either.

The girl shrugged and looked at Ginny.

Daring her to do something, really.

Ginny was tired of the attitude.
If she'd been twenty years younger she might have
taken steps towards her
and raised a hand.
Not to actually clip her one, but just
to let her see, let her see that Ginny meant business.

But she was too
slow
for nonsense like that now.

Ginny would never have imagined sleep could be possible with a
daughter away,
away in the world, and no idea where she'd gone.
But they slept.
It was one way to escape.

She'd left a note, which didn't say
enough.
There were letters in the post, and later there were photographs.
She wanted them to know she was okay.
She looked happy. She was
happy
without them.

That was difficult.

The police said there was nothing they could do, once the letters
arrived.
If she's safe and well and she doesn't want to come home, they said,

there's nothing we can do.

They were embarrassed, honestly. Ashamed.
They didn't like the thought of what people would say.
They felt rejected.
They were worried that people would think they must
have been terrible parents,
for their daughter to just
leave, like that.

So they didn't tell anyone.

They said she'd gone to London, to work.
They said she was staying with a cousin of Jacek's.
They changed the subject when it came up.

It seems ludicrous, now. But
they thought she'd be back.

People must have known
something wasn't right.
But people don't pry.

The letters kept coming, and the photographs. Always with different postmarks.

Later, when they thought about moving house, they didn't dare.
She wouldn't know
where to send the letters,
they thought.

There hasn't been a new picture for six years now,
but there will be. Laura won't let her down.
She has her own life. Ginny can be happy for her.

She probably has children, now.
A child.
It's impossible to know, but it seems likely.

She wonders, sometimes, whether having a child
would make Laura want to come back.

She has pictured it,
sometimes.

Laura
at the front door,
with a pram.
Or holding a baby.
Smiling. Apologizing.
Asking if she could come in.

Or with an older child, the two of them
holding hands.
The child too shy to talk to Ginny, at first.

Or the child grown old enough to
ask questions, to
want answers, to
make her own way to Ginny's house.

A strange child standing at the door.

So, of course.
When Ginny saw this girl in the garden,
under the apple tree.
She did wonder.

The girl had so much of Laura about her.

*

She'd asked her to leave, but
she wanted her to say who she was.
She wanted to know who she was.

So she kept her talking.

She asked how she liked the apple, and
the girl shrugged.
She told her she'd picked it a bit early, and it would likely be sour.
The girl shrugged.
She asked if she'd hurt herself coming over the fence.
The girl shrugged again.
Doesn't it hurt your shoulders, Ginny asked; all that shrugging?

The girl was trying not to smile, Ginny could see.

Ginny asked if she lived locally, knowing full well that she didn't.
I'm here on holiday, she said.
Because I don't know what it's like where you live, Ginny told her,
but in these parts people think it bad manners to go climbing over
other people's fences.

Okay, the girl said.
It sounded as close as she would ever get to an apology.
It was enough for Ginny.

When you leave, she said, I'd prefer you to go out through the front gate here. Like a normal person.

The girl did smile then, finally.

Ginny asked if her parents knew where she was.

The girl said her parents wouldn't worry about her for a few hours. She said they knew it was safe around here, and they trusted her. She was very sure of herself.

Will you know how to get back? Ginny asked. The girl nodded. She stood up, brushing herself off and picking up a bag she'd been sitting on.

My name's Becky, she said, holding out her hand.

Ginny unlocked the front gate, and told her to get a move on. Becky squeezed past her, and mumbled something that may have been thank you. Or may not.

Up close, she'd looked nothing like Laura at all.

But she'd had that spirit.

Ginny wanted to tell the girl's parents something about this. One day. She wasn't sure it would help. But she thought they might like to know.

If their girl had gone off
the way Laura did, she'd be,
she'd probably be
okay, Ginny thought.
She was younger than Laura had been
when she left,

but even so.
She'd seemed mature.
She'd seemed sensible.

They live their own lives in the end, no matter what you do.

She'd be okay.
She wanted the parents to know.

14: Jess

Whenever she'd been unfaithful, Jess would prepare a special dinner for herself and Stuart, to make up for it. He didn't know this, of course, but it made her feel as though amends were being made.

She didn't think *unfaithful* was even quite the right word. Strictly speaking, yes, that's what it was. But it wasn't disloyal. It came from a place of deep loyalty to Stuart, if anything. It was a way of ensuring their marriage could continue.

It was never difficult to arrange. Men were easy to read, and would always say yes if she asked them directly. They accepted the terms as she set them out: once only, no talking about it afterwards, total discretion. It was never thoughtless or casual, and mostly extremely pleasant. She enjoyed the anticipation she felt, and the anticipation she saw someone else feeling. The sense of two people stoking a hunger that was bigger than both of them. She enjoyed the raw abandon she felt in a strange bed. Stuart would be hurt if he ever found out, obviously, but she knew that he'd be far more hurt if she left him for the sake of this one thing. It was just a particular form of aerobic exercise, when it came down to it. What sort of a person would break up a marriage for that? It seemed as reckless as leaving someone because they didn't like playing cricket, or because they'd hung their rowing boat in the shed twenty years ago and not taken it down since.

So it was never guilt that she felt afterwards, exactly. But it did create an uncomfortable feeling of wanting to reconnect, and cooking for him was the best way she knew of doing that.

Tonight's dinner was going to be a particularly elaborate affair.

*

The girls were staying at a friend's house, and Stuart had been out at a meeting all afternoon, so she'd had plenty of time to prepare. He was late getting back, but it was probably too soon to worry. He'd gone to settle some business with Woods. The dinner would be a surprise.

Or should that be Mr. Woods? She wasn't sure if it was a surname or a nickname or even his name at all. It was one of those questions you didn't ask. Some people would be apprehensive about meeting a man like that in the first place, but Stuart had said there was no need to worry. It was all a simple misunderstanding, he'd said.

She chopped some more garlic, and added it to a salad dressing, along with fresh oregano and a splash of lemon juice.

He'd worked hard on the meeting all the same: Land Registry paperwork, a legal opinion, existing contracts. Might as well get this thing resolved in one hit, he'd said. He'd been working hard on everything lately. Things had been getting tight, business-wise.

She weighed out the bulgur wheat and put it to soak. She covered the bowl with the tea towel they'd bought when they'd gone to Morocco. That was years ago, before the children. She poured herself a glass of wine. She checked on the lamb.

The meeting was about money. Most of their problems this year had been money-related. Woods kept some mobile homes on a strip of land fronting a timber yard that Stuart had recently bought, and had apparently always been paid an access charge by the previous owner. This wasn't mentioned in the sale documents, and seemed to have no legal basis. It wasn't even clear that he owned the land his caravans were on. It was a nonsense, Stuart had said.

The timber yard had belonged to Patrick Harris, who had died a few years ago. Cathy Harris hadn't wanted to sell, but Stuart had offered her a good price. There'd been some bad feeling about it in the village, which Jess hardly thought was fair. It was a good price. But Cathy had seemed rather stilted the last few times Jess had seen her.

The lamb shoulder had been marinating since the night before. She'd waited for Stuart to go to bed, and then scored deep lines through the fat and rubbed it all over with olive oil, garlic, rosemary, and crushed juniper. When she'd got into bed he'd told her she smelled nice, wrinkling his nose in that utterly puzzled way she found so affecting. She'd left the lamb hidden at the back of the larder until he'd gone to the meeting, and then blasted it for half an hour before turning the oven down as low as it could go.

She'd never met Woods, but she knew him by reputation. Most people did, around here. Cathy had once told her he was involved in illegal gambling, and Martin at the butcher's shop changed the subject whenever his name came up. He seemed to be a kind of bogeyman figure, but there were very few specifics. It was simple reputation management, Stuart said. A type of business strategy. A face-to-face conversation would resolve the issue. He would be reasonable about it, Stuart was sure.

She laid the table. She'd ironed the tablecloth, and was using the heavy cutlery his parents had left them with the house. She'd polished the glasses, and put the wine out. She arranged some ivy around the good candlesticks, and laid out the napkins.

*

She checked the time. He really was late now. She popped outside for a moment, on the off-chance she might see his headlights along the road. It was cold and there was a thin coating of frost across the gravel. It was a cloudy night and the darkness felt close. The barn conversions across the yard were a silhouette against the darker hills beyond. The lights from the village seemed a long way off. There were no cars on the road.

Tomorrow she would put the lights on in the barn conversion, when she went over to air the rooms ready for the Shaw family's arrival. This time of year could be dank even in the middle of the day, and she wanted them to feel welcome. She knew they'd been in two minds about coming at all. She was looking forward to seeing them again, and she wanted it to go well.

They'd come for a fortnight back in August, with their daughter, Becky. She'd invited them as a test run, before they opened the new holiday lets to paying guests. The whole building process had been so fraught with cock-ups and delays, and they wanted to be sure everything was finally working properly. And the Shaws had been happy to act as guinea pigs. They were old friends, from university days. It had been good to see them again. They'd seemed to unwind over the course of the time they were here. And Becky had made friends in the village. Jess had even picked up, from her older daughter, that there was some kind of infatuation between Becky and the Broads' son, James, although what that really meant at the age of thirteen was anyone's guess.

Money had been tight, the last few years. The barn conversions were supposed to work towards solving that, as was the acquisition of the timber yard, but so far they were just deeper into debt than ever. And this business with Woods had stopped them being able to use the timber yard at all.

She went back inside and checked on the roast potatoes. They were barely golden, and just beginning to crisp. She tossed them around in the pan and put them back in the oven. The sticky smell of caramelizing garlic made her think, as it sometimes did, of their honeymoon in Greece. Everything they'd eaten there had been laced with garlic and dripping with oil, and they'd got very messy. They'd spent most of their time eating it half-naked. She'd thought, then, that their appetites would never be sated.

She didn't know what had changed, for Stuart. Something just seemed to have switched off for him, physically. He was affectionate in other ways, and they still felt close, but there was just this one lack. He wouldn't discuss it, and didn't even seem very concerned. It had nearly broken the two of them apart, until eventually she had decided that she wouldn't let it, and taken the necessary steps.

*

She set out the fish platter, letting it come back up to room temperature. She'd picked up a couple of small trout from the river keeper, who seemed to feel he owed them because the river ran past their property. She liked to fillet them thinly and leave them sitting in lemon juice and wine vinegar for a while, so the flesh had already begun to whiten before she gave them just a hint of heat and set them melting on the plate. Some roughly ground salt. A few cracked flakes of chili.

The house was quiet, without the girls around. She had a feeling of things being muffled.

She poured another glass of wine, and opened the front door again. The air was sharp, but it came as a relief after the heat of the kitchen. The clouds had thinned and the stars were coming out. She could see the long ridge of Black Bull Hill away to the left of the village lights. And in the distance, from somewhere near the visitor center, she saw headlights. This would be Stuart, now. He would be okay. She'd known he would be, really. Even with all the talk about Woods, she'd known that Stuart was in no actual danger, no actual physical danger. The man could be unpleasant and stubborn, by all accounts, but this was hardly Sicily. They weren't talking about broken fingers or kneecaps. She watched the headlights getting closer, and heard the click of the security gates unlocking at the bottom of the drive. She stepped back inside, so that he wouldn't see her watching and think she'd been worried.

He had this way of holding her, whenever he came home, just tightly enough and for long enough that she would know things were fine with them both. He did this, and kissed the top of her head. He went straight through to the kitchen and started washing his hands. She followed him.

Are you hungry? she asked. I've made a spot of dinner. The girls are staying at the Smiths'. I thought we could make an evening of it.

Lovely, he said. Lovely. He was washing his hands very thoroughly, the water steaming hot. She took the last few things out of the oven and carried them through to the dining room. She fiddled with the arrangement of the dishes and the cutlery, straightening the cloth and napkins and lighting the candles. She poured the wine, and carried the glasses back into the kitchen. Stuart was still washing his hands, but as she came into the room he turned the tap off suddenly and reached for a towel. He'd splashed water across his face as well, and for a moment he buried his face in the towel and kept it hidden.

Wine? she said, waiting.

He lowered the towel and hung it carefully on its rail. He took the glass from her, and smiled, and followed her through to the dining room. It must have been a long meeting, she guessed. He looked tired. He glanced at all the food spread out across the table. It looked like enough for half a dozen people.

You've certainly been busy, he said. There's not an occasion I've forgotten about, is there? We're not expecting anyone else?

No, she said. No one else. Just us.

Great, he said. Great. Well, thanks for this. Looks lovely. Shall we tuck in?

Stuart, she said. Is it sorted?

He was holding his hands together on the table in front of him. He couldn't keep them still. He couldn't look her in the eye.

We'll pay what he's asking, he said.

15: Joe

Once they'd agreed to get a divorce, they went back to bed. Which was rather unexpected.

They'd lingered over breakfast, and were still wearing their pajamas, and the rain against the windows was making them feel cold. And they were supposed to be on holiday, after all.

It was awkward at first. They weren't sure how close they should let themselves be. But then Charlotte reached out and took Joe's hand, and they both relaxed. It had taken them a long time to reach this decision, and by now there was no anger left in them. Only a sense of letting something go, together.

Go on, then, he said. You can tell me now. What's the one thing that's always annoyed you about me, that you've never said?

She didn't have to think for very long.

That way you squint when you don't understand something, she told him. It makes you look furious. It's very off-putting. You're doing it now.

He tried to relax his face, but apparently that only made it worse.

I think it's just the light, he told her. My eyes are very sensitive to the light.

It makes you look as though you think everyone else is stupid, she told him. You might want to work on that.

I'll make a note, he said.

You did it the very first time we met, she said. I thought you didn't like me.

The sun was in my eyes, he told her. You were sitting right in front of the sun, I could hardly see you.

You were dazzled by my beauty, you mean? she asked.

Something like that, he said.

*

They'd met by chance, outside a café where Charlotte was having breakfast with a mutual friend. She was a little hungover, and not completely listening when her friend saw him across the road and called him over. His handshake was damp, and his face started to flush as her friend introduced them. It was a hot morning, and he must have been in a rush. There were no chairs free, so her friend insisted Joe take hers. She had to get on anyway, she said, and left the two of them on their own. There was an awkward silence for a moment, and then Joe asked what she recommended for breakfast. It depended how hungry he was, Charlotte said. Oh, I'm always hungry, he'd told her.

*

That was a bit much, she told him now. I nearly wrote you off at that point.

I don't blame you, he said. I was so embarrassed, I nearly walked away myself.

What stopped you?

I was actually genuinely hungry, he said, pretending to pull away as she pretended to punch him in the shoulder.

*

The whole thing had been a setup, of course. He'd never told her this, as such. He assumed it was implicitly understood. Not acknowledging it was part of the charm, he thought. He was only a couple of years out of university, and stuck in a bit of a rut. There'd been an untidy split with a previous girlfriend. His friend Jess had taken him under her wing, and made him into a project of sorts, and this introduction was the culmination of all her work. Just come and say hello, she said; be nice, see what happens. No pressure.

This was after weeks of her coming around to make sure he was out of bed, bringing him job applications, cooking him dinner, and listening to his long explanations of why his particular heartbreak was unique before saying yes, okay, but now you must live. She even started making adjustments to his wardrobe, his hairstyle, to the way he did or didn't hold eye contact while he spoke to her. For a brief, exhilarating period he'd even thought she might be making these improvements for her own sake.

The second time they met, Charlotte had known she was being set up, and she didn't mind at all. Jess had told her plenty about Joe by then, and she'd liked what she heard. He sounded like he had his act together. He sounded sensible. She was ready for that, after a series of men who'd been anything but. She went back to his flat at the end of the evening, and stayed all weekend, and on the Monday morning she told him that she already knew she wanted to make something of it. You make me feel safe, she said. You hardly know me, he objected. I'm a good judge of character, she told him.

*

You realize that "safe" always sounded like a euphemism for boring? he said, now.

It's not the same thing at all, she said, moving closer towards him. She pressed her face into his neck and almost without thinking began to kiss his collarbone. She stopped, and pulled back, and they both looked at each other.

This was confusing.

*

Moving to London had been her idea. He was never keen, but he kept that to himself. The arrangements were in hand before they'd had a chance to discuss it. Charlotte's department was keen for her to take a transfer, and the job he'd been offered was surprisingly well paid. He would have liked to talk to Jess about it, but they'd drifted apart once he'd started seeing Charlotte, and since getting engaged. So he went ahead and tagged along to London, thinking they might come back north after a few years, or even that the relationship might anyway run its natural course. Instead, right around the time she'd started talking about marriage, Charlotte got pregnant and everything changed. They'd barely found their feet in London, and were still too young, he thought. But how did this happen? he asked her. Oh, I don't know, she said. Probably the usual way, I should think.

*

Do you think this was all a mistake? he asked her. The rain was beating hard against the window now, and the light in the room was gray and low.

No, she said, with her hand against his cheek. We were young. It wasn't a mistake. But we're older now.

She looked at him, and leaned closer, and they kissed. It was the first time they had kissed like this for months. Their mouths opened and their bodies shuffled closer together. It was so easy.

She leaned her face away from him for a moment, trying to ask him a question with her eyes.

You're squinting at me, he said. You should really learn to stop doing that.

She laughed.

*

When the midwife passed Charlotte the baby, its eyes squinted up at her in the same way that Joe's always did. It's a girl, she heard the midwife say. Hello, Rebecca, she said softly. What a pleasure to meet you. The baby said nothing, but just carried on squinting at her, looking somehow perplexed, or annoyed.

She'd been annoyed with them about a lot of things, lately. She was thirteen now, so it seemed almost natural. She was annoyed when they asked her questions about her friends, or about how she was feeling. She was annoyed when they asked why she was late getting home. She was annoyed when they asked why she'd been getting in trouble at school, or not going to school at all, and she was even annoyed when they asked her to stop slamming the door because the paint was coming away from the frame.

She'd been a lovely child for most of her life. This was just the way teenagers would become, they'd assumed; but not Becky, not this soon.

They thought their relationship had come through various stresses well enough, but they realized this was the first real challenge they'd been up against. And as it turned out, they weren't up to it. Joe in particular found himself struggling to cope with the frustration he felt towards his daughter's moods, biting his tongue and then taking it out on Charlotte. There were a series of quite unpleasant scenes.

The holiday last summer was supposed to have been their chance to reconcile, although by the time they'd got there it was already starting to feel like it might be too late. Jess had got back in touch, and invited them to come and stay; she and her husband, Stuart, had converted some barns on their land into holiday cottages, and they needed someone to test them out. Joe hadn't been at all sure if it was a good idea. He was uncomfortable about seeing Jess again, besides anything else. But Charlotte had liked the notion of a country break. Fresh air, she'd said. Long walks. Give Becky a chance to learn about nature.

As it happened, Becky had made friends with Jess and Stuart's daughter Sophie and spent most of her time mooching around in the games shed or down at the village tearoom. But there had been no slammed doors, and the breathing space had been enough for him and Charlotte to remember what it was they liked about each other. By the end of the fortnight they'd already decided to come back for a New Year's break, and they both felt that something had changed for the better between them; that they understood each other more clearly and would find a way to work out their differences. The unspoken suggestion that they might not make it, as a couple, seemed to have been left behind.

*

Just to be clear, she said. This isn't changing anything, is it?

He looked at her, trying not to squint. His pajama trousers were already down to his knees.

I mean, no, I don't think so, he said. Is it? Does it?

No, she said. But I'd like to carry on.

She slipped her pajama trousers to her ankles and kicked them to the bottom of the bed. She pulled him in towards her, feeling his old familiar willingness between her hands. She drew him all the way in. They'd stopped kissing. He was resting his forehead against her shoulder, rocking his hips gently back and forth as much from old habit as anything else.

*

When they came back in the winter the cottage felt smaller than they'd remembered. They'd imagined long bracing walks in crisp snow, but it had just rained endlessly and they were mostly stuck indoors. They almost hadn't come at all. Things had been tense between them all autumn and they were on the verge of a decision. But Becky had kept in touch with Sophie after the summer, and was desperate to see her again. So they'd driven north, bringing all the Christmas leftovers and half a case of good wine, and over breakfast on the second morning they'd agreed they would get a divorce.

Becky had been up early, and gone across the yard to spend the morning with Sophie. There had been talk of going out for a walk, but the rain was so heavy that they'd agreed to leave it until later. They'd taken their time over breakfast, and the subject of their separation had come up only gradually, and they'd both been surprised by how easy it was. It came as a relief to them both.

They agreed to talk to Becky about it later, when they went out for their walk.

*

They were still moving carefully together when Charlotte noticed that the light in the room had brightened, and the rain stopped. She turned towards the window, and they both stilled. Neither of them had yet finished, and it didn't seem necessary now.

Looks like it's clearing up, she said.

He nodded. They slipped apart. Think we can talk her into that walk, maybe after lunch? he asked.

I think we can try, she said.

They showered, and dressed, and went downstairs to look for Becky.

Acknowledgments

Barbara Crossley, Benjamin Johncock, Chris Power, Di Speirs, Edward Hogan, Éireann Lorsung, Erin Kottke, Gillian Roberts, Helen Garnons-Williams, Jane Chapman, Jenn Ashworth, Jin Auh, John McGhee, Jonathan Lee, Julian Humphries, Justine Willett, Melissa Harrison, Michelle Kane, Peak District National Park Media Centre, Richard Birkin, *Rosie Garton*, Sarah Hall, Tracy Bohan, Wah-Ming Chang.